Marx Joyce Abbott Hardy Montaigne Machiavelli Chesterton Cooper Emerson Austen Defoe Melville Haggard Hugo Christie Carroll Eliot Grimm Stoker Molière Wilde Maupassant Byron Schiller Garnett Einstein Fitzgerald Engels Smith Kafka Goethe Hawthorne Dostoyevsky Hall Cotton Baum Kipling Doyle Willis Leslie Dumas Henry Nietzsche Flaubert Turgenev Balzac Stockton Vatsyayana Crane Burroughs Verne Curtis Tocqueville Whitman Gogol Vinci Homer Widger Tolstoy Busch Darwin Thoreau Scott Potter Freud Zola Lawrence Twain Plato Kant Jowett Stevenson Dickens Andersen Burton Hesse Harte London Descartes Cervantes Poe Aristotle Wells Voltaire Hale James Hastings Cooke Bunner Shakespeare Richter Chekhov Chambers Irving Doré da Swift Dante Shaw Wodehouse Benedict Alcott Pushkin Newton tredition®

tredition was established in 2006 by Sandra Latusseck and Soenke Schulz. Based in Hamburg, Germany, tredition offers publishing solutions to authors and publishing houses, combined with worldwide distribution of printed and digital book content. tredition is uniquely positioned to enable authors and publishing houses to create books on their own terms and without conventional manufacturing risks.

For more information please visit: www.tredition.com

TREDITION CLASSICS

This book is part of the TREDITION CLASSICS series. The creators of this series are united by passion for literature and driven by the intention of making all public domain books available in printed format again - worldwide. Most TREDITION CLASSICS titles have been out of print and off the bookstore shelves for decades. At tredition we believe that a great book never goes out of style and that its value is eternal. Several mostly non-profit literature projects provide content to tredition. To support their good work, tredition donates a portion of the proceeds from each sold copy. As a reader of a TREDITION CLASSICS book, you support our mission to save many of the amazing works of world literature from oblivion. See all available books at www.tredition.com.

Project Gutenberg

The content for this book has been graciously provided by Project Gutenberg. Project Gutenberg is a non-profit organization founded by Michael Hart in 1971 at the University of Illinois. The mission of Project Gutenberg is simple: To encourage the creation and distribution of eBooks. Project Gutenberg is the first and largest collection of public domain eBooks.

The Law and the Word

T. (Thomas) Troward

Imprint

This book is part of TREDITION CLASSICS

Author: T. (Thomas) Troward
Cover design: Buchgut, Berlin – Germany

Publisher: tredition GmbH, Hamburg - Germany
ISBN: 978-3-8424-7875-6

www.tredition.com
www.tredition.de

CONTENTS

CHAPTER

FOREWORD

I SOME FACTS IN NATURE

II SOME PSYCHIC EXPERIENCES

III MAN'S PLACE IN THE CREATIVE ORDER

IV THE LAW OF WHOLENESS

V THE SOUL OF THE SUBJECT

VI THE PROMISES

VII DEATH AND IMMORTALITY

VIII TRANSFERRING THE BURDEN

FOOTNOTES:

FOREWORD

THOMAS TROWARD
AN APPRECIATION

How is one to know a friend? Certainly not by the duration of acquaintance. Neither can friendship be bought or sold by service rendered. Nor can it be coined into acts of gallantry or phrases of flattery. It has no part in the small change of courtesy. It is outside all these, containing them all and superior to them all.

To some is given the great privilege of a day set apart to mark the arrival of a total stranger panoplied with all the insignia of friendship. He comes unannounced. He bears no letter of introduction. No mutual friend can vouch for him. Suddenly and silently he steps unexpectedly out of the shadow of material concern and spiritual obscurity, into the radiance of intimate friendship, as a picture is projected upon a lighted screen. But unlike the phantom picture he is an instant reality that one's whole being immediately recognizes, and the radiance of fellowship that pervades his word, thought and action holds all the essence of long companionship.

Unfortunately there are too few of these bright messengers of God to be met with in life's pilgrimage, but that Judge Troward was one of them will never be doubted by the thousands who are now mourning his departure from among us. Those whose closest touch with him has been the reading of his books will mourn him as a friend only less than those who listened to him on the platform. For no books ever written more clearly expressed the author. The same simple lucidity and gentle humanity, the same effort to discard complicated non-essentials, mark both the man and his books.

Although the spirit of benign friendliness pervades his writings and illuminated his public life, yet much of his capacity for friendship was denied those who were not privileged to clasp hands with him and to sit beside him in familiar confidence. Only in the intimacy of the fireside did he wholly reveal his innate modesty and simplicity of character. Here alone, glamoured with his radiating friendship, was shown the wealth of his richly-stored mind equipped by nature and long training to deal logically with the most profound and abstruse questions of life. Here indeed was proof of his greatness, his unassuming superiority, his humanity, his keen sense of honour, his wit and humour, his generosity and all the characteristics of a rare gentleman, a kindly philosopher and a true friend.

To Judge Troward was given the logician's power to strip a subject bare of all superfluous and concealing verbiage, and to exhibit the gleaming jewels of truth and reality in splendid simplicity. This supreme quality, this ability to make the complex simple, the power to subordinate the non-essential, gave to his conversation, to his lectures, to his writings, and in no less degree to his personality, a direct and charming naïveté that at once challenged attention and compelled confidence and affection.

His sincerity was beyond question. However much one might differ from him in opinion, at least one never doubted his profound faith and complete devotion to truth. His guileless nature was beyond ungenerous suspicions and selfish ambitions. He walked calmly upon his way wrapped in the majesty of his great thoughts, oblivious to the vexations of the world's cynicism. Charity and reverence for the indwelling spirit marked all his human relations. Tolerance of the opinions of others, benevolence and tenderness dwelt in his every word and act. Yet his careful consideration of others did not paralyze the strength of his firm will or his power to strike hard blows at wrong and error. The search for truth, to which his life was devoted, was to him a holy quest. That he could and would lay a lance in defence of his opinions is evidenced in his writings, and has many times been demonstrated to the discomfiture of assailing critics. But his urbanity was a part of himself and never departed from him.

Not to destroy but to create was his part in the world. In developing his philosophy he built upon the foundation of his predecessors. No good and true stone to be found among the ruins of the past, but was carefully worked into his superstructure of modern thought, radiant with spirituality, to the building of which the enthusiasm of his life was devoted.

To one who has studied Judge Troward, and grasped the significance of his theory of the "Universal Sub-conscious Mind," and who also has attained to an appreciation of Henri Bergson's theory of a "Universal Livingness," superior to and outside the material Universe, there must appear a distinct correlation of ideas. That intricate and ponderously irrefutable argument that Bergson has so patiently built up by deep scientific research and unsurpassed profundity of thought and crystal-clear reason, that leads to the substantial conclusion that man has leapt the barrier of materiality only by the urge of some external pressure superior to himself, but which, by reason of infinite effort, he alone of all terrestrial beings has succeeded in utilizing in a superior manner and to his advantage: this well-rounded and exhaustively demonstrated argument in favour of a super-livingness in the universe, which finds its highest terrestrial expression in man, appears to be the scientific demonstration of Judge Troward's basic principle of the "Universal Sub-conscious Mind." This universal and infinite God-consciousness which Judge Troward postulates as man's sub-consciousness, and from which man was created and is maintained, and of which all physical, mental and spiritual manifestation is a form of expression, appears to be a corollary of Bergson's demonstrated "Universal Livingness." What Bergson has so brilliantly proven by patient and exhaustive processes of science, Judge Troward arrived at by intuition, and postulated as the basis of his argument, which he proceeded to develop by deductive reasoning.

The writer was struck by the apparent parallelism of these two distinctly dissimilar philosophies, and mentioned the discovery to Judge Troward who naturally expressed a wish to read Bergson, with whose writings he was wholly unacquainted. A loan of Bergson's "Creative Evolution" produced no comment for several weeks, when it was returned with the characteristic remark, "I've tried my best to get hold of him, but I don't know what he is talking about." I mention the remark as being characteristic only because it indicates his extreme modesty and disregard of exhaustive scientific research.

The Bergson method of scientific expression was unintelligible to his mind, trained to intuitive reasoning. The very elaborateness and microscopic detail that makes Bergson great is opposed to Judge Troward's method of simplicity. He cared not for complexities, and the intricate minutiæ of the process of creation, but was only concerned with its motive power—the spiritual principles upon which it was organized and upon which it proceeds.

Although the conservator of truth of every form and degree wherever found, Judge Troward was a ruthless destroyer of sham and pretence. To those submissive minds that placidly accept everything indiscriminately, and also those who prefer to follow along paths of well-beaten opinion, because the beaten path is popular, to all such he would perhaps appear to be an irreverent iconoclast seeking to uproot long accepted dogma and to overturn existing faiths. Such an opinion of Judge Troward's work could not prevail with any one who has studied his teachings.

His reverence for the fundamental truths of religious faith was profound, and every student of his writings will testify to the great constructive value of his work. He builded upon an ancient foundation a new and nobler structure of human destiny, solid in its simplicity and beautiful in its innate grandeur.

But to the wide circle of Judge Troward's friends he will best and most gloriously be remembered as a teacher. In his magic mind the unfathomable revealed its depths and the illimitable its boundaries; metaphysics took on the simplicity of the ponderable, and man himself occupied a new and more dignified place in the Cosmos. Not only did he perceive clearly, but he also possessed that quality of mind even more rare than deep and clear perception, that clarity of expression and exposition that can carry another and less-informed mind along with it, on the current of its understanding, to a logical and comprehended conclusion.

In his books, his lectures and his personality he was always ready to take the student by the hand, and in perfect simplicity and friendliness to walk and talk with him about the deeper mysteries of life—the life that includes death—and to shed the brilliant light of his wisdom upon the obscure and difficult problems that torment sincere but rebellious minds.

His artistic nature found expression in brush and canvas and his great love for the sea is reflected in many beautiful marine sketches. But if painting was his recreation, his work was the pursuit of Truth wherever to be found, and in whatever disguise.

His life has enriched and enlarged the lives of many, and all those who knew him will understand that in helping others he was accomplishing exactly what he most desired. Knowledge, to him, was worth only what it yielded in uplifting humanity to a higher spiritual appreciation, and to a deeper understanding of God's purpose and man's destiny.

A man, indeed! He strove not for a place,
Nor rest, nor rule. He daily walked with God.
His willing feet with service swift were shod—
An eager soul to serve the human race,
Illume the mind, and fill the heart with grace—
Hope blooms afresh where'er those feet have trod.
PAUL DERRICK.

THE LAW AND THE WORD

CHAPTER I

SOME FACTS IN NATURE

If I were asked what, in my opinion, distinguishes the thought of the present day from that of a previous generation, I should feel inclined to say, it is the fact that people are beginning to realize that Thought is a power in itself, one of the great forces of the Universe, and ultimately the greatest of forces, directing all the others. This idea seems to be, as the French say, "in the air," and this very well expresses the state of the case—the idea is rapidly spreading through many countries and through all classes, but it is still very much "in the air." It is to a great extent as yet only in a gaseous condition, vague and nebulous, and so not leading to the practical results, both individual and collective, which might be expected of it, if it were consolidated into a more workable form. We are like some amateurs who want to paint finished pictures before they have studied the elements of Art, and when they see an artist do without difficulty what they vainly attempt, they look upon him as a being specially favoured by Providence, instead of putting it down to their own want of knowledge. The idea is true. Thought *is* the great power of the Universe. But to make it practically available we must know something of the principles by which it works—that it is not a mere vaporous indefinable influence floating around and subject to no known laws, but that on the contrary, it follows laws as uncompromising as those of mathematics, while at the same time allowing unlimited freedom to the individual.

Now the purpose of the following pages, is to suggest to the reader the lines on which to find his way out of this nebulous sort of thought into something more solid and reliable. I do not profess, like a certain Negro preacher, to "unscrew the inscrutable," for we can never reach a point where we shall not find the inscrutable still ahead of us; but if I can indicate the use of a screw-driver instead of a hatchet, and that the screws should be turned from left to right, instead of from right to left, it may enable us to unscrew some things which would otherwise remain screwed down tight. We are all beginners, and indeed the hopefulness of life is in realizing that there are such vistas of unending possibilities before us, that however far we may advance, we shall always be on the threshold of something greater. We must be like Peter Pan, the boy who never grew up—heaven defend me from ever feeling quite grown up, for then I should come to a standstill; so the reader must take what I have to say simply as the talk of one boy to another in the Great School, and not expect too much.

The first question then is, where to begin. Descartes commenced his book with the words "Cogito, ergo sum." "I think, therefore I am," and we cannot do better than follow his example. There are two things about which we cannot have any doubt—our own existence, and that of the world around us. But what is it in us that is aware of these two things, that hopes and fears and plans regarding them? Certainly not our flesh and bones. A man whose leg has been amputated is able to think just the same. Therefore it is obvious that there is something in us which receives impressions and forms ideas, that reasons upon facts and determines upon courses of action and carries them out, which is not the physical body. This is the real "I Myself." This is the Person we are really concerned with; and it is the betterment of this "I Myself" that makes it worth while to enquire what our Thought has to do in the matter.

Equally true it is on the other hand that the forces of Nature around us do not think. Steam, electricity, gravitation, and chemical affinity do not think. They follow certain fixed laws which we have no power to alter. Therefore we are confronted at the outset by a broad distinction between two modes of Motion—the Movement of Thought and the Movement of Cosmic Energy—the one based upon the exercise of Consciousness and Will, and the other based upon Mathematical Sequence. This is why that system of instruction known as Free Masonry starts by erecting the two symbolic pillars Jachin and Boaz—Jachin so called from the root "Yak" meaning "One," indicating the Mathematical element of Law; and Boaz, from the root "Awáz" meaning "Voice" indicating Personal element of Free Will. These names are taken from the description in I Kings vii, 21 and II Chron. iii, 17 of the building of Solomon's Temple, where these two pillars stood before the entrance, the meaning being that the Temple of Truth can only be entered by passing between them, that is, by giving each of these factors their due relation to the other, and by realizing that they are the two Pillars of the Universe, and that no real progress can be made except by finding the true balance between them. Law and Personality—these are the two great principles with which we have to deal, and the problem is to square the one with the other.

Let me start, then, by considering some well established facts in the physical world which show how the known Law acts under certain known conditions, and this will lead us on in an intelligible manner to see how the same Law is likely to work under as yet unknown conditions. If we had to deal with unknown laws as well as unknown conditions we should, indeed, be up a gum tree. Fancy a mathematician having to solve an equation, both sides of which were entirely made up of unknown quantities—where would he be? Happily this is not the case. The Law is ONE throughout, and the apparent variety of its working results from the infinite variety of the conditions under which it may work. Let us lay a foundation, then, by seeing how it works in what we call the common course of Nature. A few examples will suffice.

Hardly more than a generation ago it was supposed that the analysis of matter could not be carried further than its reduction to some seventy primary chemical elements, which in various combinations produced all material substances; but there was no explanation how all these different elements came into existence. Each appeared to be an original creation, and there was no accounting for them. But now-a-days, as the rustic physician says in Molière's play of the "Médecin Malgré Lui," "nous avons changé tout cela." Modern science has shown conclusively that every kind of chemical atom is composed of particles of one original substance which appears to pervade all space, and to which the name of Ether has been given. Some of these particles carry a positive charge of electricity and some a negative, and the chemical atom is formed by the grouping of a certain number of negatively charged particles round a centre composed of positive electricity around which they revolve; and it is the number of these particles and the rate of their motion that determines the nature of the atom, whether, for instance, it will be an atom of iron or an atom of hydrogen, and thus we are brought back to Plato's old aphorism that the Universe consists of Number and Motion.

The size of these etheric particles is small beyond anything but abstract mathematical conception. Sir Oliver Lodge is reported to have made the following comparison in a lecture delivered at Birmingham. "The chemical atom," he said, "is as small in comparison to a drop of water as a cricket-ball is compared to the globe of the earth; and yet this atom is as large in comparison to one of its constituent particles as Birmingham town-hall is to a pin's head." Again, it has been said that in proportion to the size of the particles the distance at which they revolve round the centre of the atom is as great as the distance from the earth to the sun. I must leave the realization of such infinite minuteness to the reader's imagination—it is beyond mine.

Modern science thus shows us all material substance, whether that of inanimate matter or that of our own bodies, as proceeding out of one primary etheric substance occupying all space and homogeneous, that is being of a uniform substance—and having no qualities to distinguish one part from another. Now this conclusion of science is important because it is precisely the fact that out of this homogeneous substance particles are produced which differ from the original substance in that they possess positive and negative energy and of these particles the atom is built up. So then comes the question: What started this differentiation?

The electronic theory which I have just mentioned takes us as far as a universal homogeneous ether as the source from which all matter is evolved, but it does not account for how motion originated in it; but perhaps another closely allied scientific theory will help us. Let us, then, turn to the question of Vibrations or Waves in Ether. In scientific language the length of a wave is the distance from the crest of one wave to that of the wave immediately following it. Now modern science recognizes a long series of waves in ether, commencing with the smallest yet known measuring 0.1 micron, or about 1/254,000 of an inch, in length, measured by Professor Schumann in 1893, and extending to waves of many miles in length used in wireless telegraphy—for instance those employed between Clifden in Galway and Glace Bay in Nova Scotia are estimated to have a length of nearly four miles. These infinitesimally small ultra-violet or actinic waves, as they are called, are the principal agents in photography, and the great waves of wireless telegraphy are able to carry a force across the Atlantic which can sensibly affect the apparatus on the other side; therefore we see that the ether of space affords a medium through which energy can be transmitted by means of vibrations.

But what starts the vibrations? Hertz announced his discovery of the electro-magnetic waves, now known by his name, in 1888; but, following up the labours of various other investigators, Lodge, Marconi and others finally developed their practical application after Hertz's death which occurred in 1894. To Hertz, however, belongs the honour of discovering how to generate these waves by means of sudden, sharply defined, electrical discharges. The principle may be illustrated by dropping a stone in smooth water. The sudden impact sets up a series of ripples all round the centre of disturbance, and the electrical impulse acts similarly in the ether. Indeed the fact that the waves flow in all directions from the central impulse is one of the difficulties of wireless telegraphy, because the message may be picked up in any direction by a receiver tuned to the same rate of vibration, and the interest for us consists in the hypothesis that thought-waves act in an analogous manner.

That vibrations are excited by sound is beautifully exemplified by the eidophone, an instrument invented, I believe, by Mrs. Watts-Hughes, and with which I have seen that lady experiment. Dry sand is scattered on a diaphragm on which the eidophone concentrates the vibrations from music played near it. The sand, as it were, dances in time to the music, and when the music stops is found to settle into definite forms, sometimes like a tree or a flower, or else some geometrical figure, but never a confused jumble. Perhaps in this we may find the origin of the legends regarding the creative power of Orpheus' lyre, and also the sacred dances of the ancients—who knows!

Perhaps some critical reader may object that sound travels by means of atmospheric and not etheric waves; but is he prepared to say that it cannot produce etheric waves also. The very recent discovery of transatlantic telephoning tends to show that etheric waves can be generated by sound, for on the 20th of October, 1915, words spoken in New York were immediately heard in Paris, and could therefore only have been transmitted through the ether, for sound travels through the atmosphere only at the rate of about 750 miles an hour, while the speed of impulses through ether can only be compared to that of light or 186,000 miles in a second. It is therefore a fair inference that etheric vibrations can be inaugurated by sound.

Perhaps the reader may feel inclined to say with the Irishman that all this is "as dry as ditch-water," but he will see before long that it has a good deal to do with ourselves. For the present what I want him to realize by a few examples is the mathematical accuracy of Law. The value of these examples lies in their illustration of the fact that the Law can always be trusted to lead us on to further knowledge. We see it working under known conditions, and relying on its unchangeableness, we can then logically infer what it will do under other hypothetical conditions, and in this way many important discoveries have been made. For instance it was in this way that Mendeléef, the Russian chemist, assumed the existence of three then unknown chemical elements, now called Scandium, Gallium and Germanium. There was a gap in the orderly sequence of the chemical elements, and relying on the old maxim—"Natura nihil facit per saltum"—Nature nowhere leaves a gap to jump over—he argued that if such elements did not exist they ought to, and so he calculated what these elements ought to be like, giving their atomic weight, chemical affinities, and the like; and when they were discovered many years later they were found to answer exactly to his description. He prophesied, not by guesswork, but by knowledge of the Law; and in much the same way radium was discovered by Professor and Madame Curie. In like manner Hertz was led to the discovery of the electro-magnetic waves. The celebrated mathematician Clerk-Maxwell had calculated all particulars of these waves twenty-five years before Hertz, on the basis of these calculations, worked out his discovery. Again, Neptune, the outermost known planet of our system was discovered by the astronomer Galle in consequence of calculations made by Leverrier. Certain variations in the movements of the planets were mathematically unaccountable except on the hypothesis that some more remote planet existed. Astronomers had faith in mathematics and the hypothetical planet was found to be a reality. Instances of this kind might be multiplied, but as the French say "à quoi bon?" I think these will be sufficient to convince the reader that the invariable sequence of Law is a factor to be relied upon, and that by studying its working under known conditions we may get at least some measure of light on conditions which are as yet unknown to us.

Let us now pass on to the human subject and consider a few examples of what is usually called the psychic side of our nature. Walt Whitman was quite right when he said that we are not all included between our hat and our boots; we shall find that our modes of consciousness and powers of action are not entirely restricted to our physical body. The importance of this line of enquiry lies in the fact that if we do possess extra-physical powers, these also form part of our personality and must be included in our estimate of our relation to our environment, and it is therefore worth our while to consider them.

Some very interesting experiments have been made by De Rochas, an eminent French scientist, which go to show that under certain magnetic conditions the sensation of physical touch can be experienced at some distance from the body. He found that under these conditions the person experimented on is insensible to the prick of a needle run into his skin, but if the prick is made about an inch-and-a-half away from the surface of the skin he feels it. Again at about three inches from this point he feels the prick of the needle, but is insensible to it in the space between these two points. Then there comes another interval in which no sensation is conveyed, but at about three inches still further away he again feels the sensation, and so on; so that he appears to be surrounded by successive zones of sensation, the first about an inch-and-a-half from the body, and the others at intervals of about three inches each. The number of these zones seems to vary in different cases, but in some there are as many as six or seven, thus giving a radius of sensation, extending to more than twenty inches beyond the body.

Now to explain this we must have recourse to what I have already said about waves. The heart and the lungs are the two centres of automatic rhythmic movement in the body, and each projects its own series of vibrations into the etheric envelope. Those projected by the lungs are estimated to be three times the length of those projected by the heart, while those projected by the heart are three times as rapid as those projected by the lungs. Consequently if the two sets of waves start together the crest of every third wave of the rapid series of short waves will coincide with the crest of one of the long waves of the slower series, while the intermediate short waves will coincide with the depression of one of the long waves. Now the effect of the crest of one wave overtaking that of another going in the same direction, is to raise the two together at that point into a single wave of greater amplitude or height than the original waves had by themselves; if the reader has the opportunity of studying the inflowing of waves on the seabeach he can verify this for himself. Consequently when the more rapid etheric waves overtake the slower ones they combine to form a larger wave, and it is at these points that the zones of sensation occur. If the reader will draw a diagram of two waved lines travelling along the same horizontal line and so proportioned that the crest of each of the large waves coincides with the crest of every third wave of the small ones, he will see what I mean: and if he then recollects that the fall in the larger waves neutralizes the rise in the smaller ones, and that because this double series starts from the interior of the body the surface of the body comes just at one of these neutralized points, he will see why sensation is neutralized there; and he will also see why the succeeding zones of sensation are double the distance from each other that the first one is from the surface of the body; it is simply because the surface of the body cuts the first long wave exactly in the middle, and therefore only half that wave occurs outside the body. This is the explanation given by De Rochas, and it affords another example of that principle of mathematical sequence of which I have spoken. It would appear that under normal conditions the double series of vibrations is spread all over the body, and so all parts are alike sensitive to touch.

I think, then, we may assume on the basis of De Rochas' experiments and others that there are such things as etheric vibrations proceeding from human personality, and in the next chapter I will give some examples showing that the psychic personality extends still further than these experiments, taken by themselves, would indicate—in fact that we possess an additional range of faculties far exceeding those which we ordinarily exercise through the physical body, and which must therefore be included in our conception of ourselves if we are to have an adequate idea of what we really are.

CHAPTER II

SOME PSYCHIC EXPERIENCES

The preceding chapter has introduced the reader to the general subject of etheric vibration as one of the natural forces of the Universe, both as the foundation of all matter and as the medium for the transmission of energy to immense distances, and also as something continually emanating from human beings. In the present chapter I shall consider it more particularly in this last aspect, which, as included in our own personality, very immediately concerns ourselves. I will commence with an instance of the practical application of this fact. Some years ago I was lunching at the house of Lady –– in company of a well-known mental healer whom I will call Mr. Y. and a well-known London physician whom I will call Dr. W. Mr. Y. mentioned the case of a lady whose leg had been amputated above the knee some years previously to her coming under his care, yet she frequently felt pains in the (amputated) knee and lower part of the left leg and foot. Dr. W. said this was to be attributed to the nerves which convey to the brain the sensation of the extremities, much as a telegraph line might be tapped in the middle, and Mr. Y. agreed that this was perfectly true on the purely physical side. But he went on to say, that accidentally putting his hand where the amputated foot should have been he felt it there. Then it occurred to him that since there was no material foot to be touched, it must be through the medium of his own psychic body that the sensation of touch was conveyed to him, and accordingly he asked the lady to imagine that she was making various movements with the amputated limb, all of which he felt, and was able to tell her what each movement was, which she said he did correctly. Then, to carry the experiment further, he reversed the process and with his hand moved the invisible leg and foot in various ways, all of which the lady felt and described. He then determined to treat the invisible leg as though it were a real one, and joined up the circuit by taking her left foot in his right hand and her right foot (the amputated one) in his left, with the result that she immediately felt relief; and after successive treatments in this way was entirely cured.

A well authenticated case like this opens up a good many interesting questions regarding the Psychic Body, but the most important point appears to me to be that we are able to experience sensation by means of it. In this case, however, and those mentioned in the preceding chapter, the physical body was actually present, and if we stopped at this point, we might question whether its presence was not a *sine qua non* for the action of the etheric vibrations. I will therefore pass on to a class of examples which show that very curious phenomena can take place without the physical body being on the spot. There are numerous well verified cases of the kind to be found in the records of the Society for Psychical Research and in other books by trustworthy writers; but it may perhaps interest the present reader to hear one or two instances of my personal experience which, though they may not be so striking as some of those recorded by others, still point in the same direction.

My first introduction to Scotland was when I delivered the course of lectures in Edinburgh which led to the publication of my first book, the "Edinburgh Lectures on Mental Science." The following years I gave a second course of lectures in Edinburgh, but the friends who had kindly entertained me on the former occasion had in the meanwhile gone to live elsewhere. However, a certain Mr. S., whose acquaintance I had made on my previous visit, invited me to stay with him for a day or two while I could look round for other accommodation, though, as it turned out, I remained at his house during the whole month I was in Edinburgh. I had, however, never seen his house, which was on the opposite side of the town to where I had stayed before. I arrived there on a Tuesday, and Mr. S. and his family at once met me with the question:

"What were you thinking of at ten o'clock on Sunday evening?"

I could not immediately recall this, and also wanted to know the reason of their question.

"We have something curious to tell you," they replied, "but first try to remember what you were thinking of at ten o'clock on Sunday evening—were you thinking about us?"

Then I recollected that about that time I was saying my usual prayers before going to bed and had asked that, if I could stay only a day or two with Mr. S., I should be directed to a suitable place for the remainder of the time.

"That explains it," they replied; and then they went on to tell me that at the hour in question Mr. S. and his son, a young man of about twenty, had entered their dining-room together and seen me standing leaning against the mantel-shelf. They were both hard-headed Scotchmen engaged in business in Edinburgh, and certainly not the sort of people to conjure up fanciful imaginings, nor is it likely that the same fancy should have occurred to both of them; and therefore I can only suppose that they actually saw what they said they did. Now I myself was in London at the time of this appearance in Edinburgh, of which I had no consciousness whatever; at the same time the fact of my being seen in Edinburgh exactly at the time when my thought, in prayer, was centred upon Mr. S.'s house (which I had not then seen) is a coincidence suggesting that in some way my Thought had made itself visible there in the image of my external personality.

In this case, as I have said, I was not conscious of my psychic visit to Edinburgh, but I will now relate a converse instance, which occurred in connection with my first visit there. At that time I had never been in Scotland, and so far as I knew was never likely to go there. I was wide awake, writing in my study at Norwood, where I then lived, when I suddenly found myself in a place totally unknown to me, where stood the ruins of an ancient abbey, part of which, however, was still roofed over and used as a place of worship. I felt much interested, and among other things I noted a Latin inscription on a tablet in one of the walls. There seemed to be an invisible guide showing me over the place, who then pointed out a long low house opposite the abbey, and said: "This is the house of the clergyman of the abbey"; and I was then taken inside the house and shown a number of antique-looking rooms. Then I came to myself, and found I was sitting at my writing-table in Norwood. I had, however, a clear recollection of the place I had seen, but no idea where it was, or indeed whether any such place really existed. I also remembered a portion of the Latin inscription, which I at once wrote down in a note-book, as my curiosity was aroused.

As I have said, I had no reason at that time to suppose I should ever go to Scotland, but some weeks later I was invited to lecture in Edinburgh. Another visitor in the house where I was a guest there, was the wife of the County Court Judge of Cumberland, and I showed her and our hostess the part of the Latin inscription I had retained, and suggested that perhaps it might exist somewhere in Edinburgh. However nothing answering to what I had seen was to be found, so we relegated the whole thing to the region of unaccountable fancies, and thought no more about it. The Judge's wife took her departure before me, and kindly invited me to spend a few days at their residence near Carlisle on my return journey, which I did. One day she drove me out to see Lanercost Abbey, one of the show-places of the neighbourhood, and walking round the building I found in one of the walls the Latin inscription in question. I called Mrs. — —, who was a little way off, and said: "Look at this inscription."

She at once replied: "Why! that is the very inscription we were all puzzling over in Edinburgh!"

It turned out to be an inscription in memory of the founder of the abbey, dating from somewhere in the eleven-hundreds. The whole place answered exactly to what I had seen, and the long low parsonage was there also.

"I should have liked you to see it inside," said Mrs. — —, "but I have never met the vicar, though I know his mother-in-law, so we must give it up."

We were just entering our carriage when the garden-gate opened, and who should come out but the mother-in-law.

"Oh, Mrs. — —," she said, addressing the Judge's wife, "I am here on a visit and you must come in and take tea." So we went in and were shown over the house, much as I had been in my vision, and some portions were so old that, among other rooms, we were shown the one occupied by King Edward I on his march against Scotland in the year 1296, when the Scottish regalia was captured, and the celebrated Crowning-Stone was brought to England and placed in Westminster Abbey, where it has ever since remained—a stone having an occult relation to the history of the British and American peoples of the highest interest to both, but as there is already an extensive literature on this subject I will not enter upon it here.

I will now relate another curious experience. We had only recently taken up our residence at Norwood, when one day I was seated in the dining-room, but suddenly found myself in the hall, and saw two ladies going up the stairs. They passed close to me, and turning round the landing at the top of the stairs passed out of sight in a perfectly natural manner. They looked as solid as any one I have ever seen in my life. One of them was a stout lady with a rather florid complexion, apparently between forty-five and fifty, wearing a silk blouse with thin purple and white stripes. Leaning on her arm was a slightly-built old lady with white ringlets, dressed all in black and wearing a lace mantilla. I noticed their appearance particularly. The next moment I found I was really sitting in the dining-room, and that the ladies I had seen were nothing but visionary figures. I wondered what it could mean, but as we had only recently taken the house, thought it better not to mention it to any of my family, for fear of causing them alarm. But a few days later I mentioned it to a Mrs. F. who I knew had had some experience in such matters, and she said: "You have seen either some one who has lived in the house or who is going to live there." Then the matter dropped.

About a month later my wife arranged by correspondence for a certain Miss B. to come as governess to our children. When she arrived there was no mistaking her identity. She was the stout lady I had seen, and the next morning she came down to breakfast dressed in the identical blouse with purple and white stripes. There was no mistaking her, but I was puzzled as to who the other figure could be whom I had seen along with her. I resolved, however, to say nothing about the matter until we became better acquainted, lest she should think that my mind was not quite balanced. I therefore held my peace for six months, at the end of which time I concluded that we knew enough of each other to allow one another credit for being fairly level-headed. Then I thought, now if I tell her what I saw she may perhaps be acted upon by suggestion and imagine a resemblance between the unknown figure and some acquaintance of hers, so I will not begin by telling her of the vision, but will first ask if she knows any one answering to the description, and give her the reason afterwards. I therefore took a suitable opportunity of asking her if she knew any such person, describing the figure to her as accurately as I could.

Her look of surprise grew as I went on, and when I had finished she explained with astonishment: "Why, Mr. Troward, where *could* you have seen my mother? She is an invalid, and I am certain you have never seen her, and yet you have described her most accurately."

Then I told her what I had seen. She asked what I thought was the explanation of the appearance, and the only explanation I could give was, that I supposed she was on the look-out for a post and paid us a preliminary visit to see whether ours would suit her, and that, being naturally interested in her welfare, her mother had accompanied her. Perhaps you will say: "What came of it?" Well, nothing "came of it," nor did anything "come" of my psychic visits to Edinburgh and Lanercost Abbey. Such occurrences seem to be simple facts in Nature which, though on some occasions connected with premonitions of more or less importance, are by no means necessarily so. They are the functioning of certain faculties which we all possess, but of the nature of which we as yet know very little.

It will be noticed that in the first of these three cases I myself was the person seen, though unaware of the fact. In the last I was the percipient, but the persons seen by me were unconscious of their visit; and in the second case I was conscious of my presence at a place which I had never heard of, and which I visited some time after. In two of these cases, therefore, the persons, making the psychic visit, were not aware of having done so, while in the third, a memory of what had been seen was retained. But all three cases have this in common, that the psychic visit was not the result of an act of conscious volition, and also, that the psychic action took place at a long distance from the physical body.

From these personal experiences, as well as from many well authenticated cases recorded by other writers, I should be inclined to infer that the psychic action is entirely independent of the physical body, and in support of this view I will cite yet another experience.

It was about the year 1875, when I was a young Assistant Commissioner in the Punjab, that I was ordered to the small up-country station of Akalpur, [1] and took possession of the Assistant Commissioner's bungalow there. On the night of our arrival in the bungalow, my wife and I had our charpoys—light Indian bedsteads—placed side by side in a certain room and went to bed. The last thing I remembered before falling asleep, was seeing my wife sitting up in bed, reading with a lamp on a small table beside her. Suddenly I was awakened by the sound of a shot, and starting up, found the room in darkness. I immediately lit a candle which was on a chair by my bedside, and found my wife still sitting up with the book on her knee, but the lamp had gone out.

"Take me away, take me into another room," she exclaimed.

"Why, what is the matter?" I said.

"Did you not see it?" she replied.

"See what?" I asked.

"Don't stop to ask any questions," she replied; "get me out of this room at once; I can't stop here another minute."

I saw she was very frightened, so I called up the servants, and had our beds removed to a room on the other side of the house, and then she told me what she had seen. She said: "I was sitting reading as you saw me, when looking round, I saw the figure of an Englishman standing close by my bedside, a fine-looking man with a large fair moustache and dressed in a grey suit. I was so surprised that I could not speak, and we remained looking at each other for about a minute. Then he bent over me and whispered: 'Don't be afraid,' and with that there was the sound of a shot, and everything was in darkness."

"My dear girl, you must have fallen asleep over your book and been dreaming," I said.

"No, I was wide awake," she insisted; "you were asleep, but I was awake all the time. But you heard the shot, did you not?"

"Yes," I replied, "that is what woke me—some one must have fired a shot outside."

"But why should any one be shooting in our garden at nearly midnight?" my wife objected.

It certain seemed strange, but it was the only explanation that suggested itself; so we had to agree to differ, she being convinced that she had seen a ghost, and that the shot had been inside the room, and I being equally convinced that she had been dreaming, and that the shot had been fired outside the house.

The next morning the owner of the bungalow, an old widow lady, Mrs. La Chaire, called to make kindly enquiries as to whether she could be of any service to us on our arrival. After thanking her, my wife said: "I expect you will laugh at me, but I cannot help telling you there is something strange about the bungalow"; and she then went on to narrate what she had seen.

Instead of laughing the old lady looked more and more serious as she went on, and when she had done asked to be shown exactly where the apparition had appeared. My wife took her to the spot, and on being shown it old Mrs. La Chaire exclaimed: "This is the most wonderful thing I have ever heard of. Eighteen years ago my bed was on the very spot where yours was last night, and I was lying in it too ill to move, when my husband, whom you have described most accurately, stood where you saw him and shot himself dead."

This statement of the widow convinced me that my wife had really seen what she said she had, and had not dreamed it; and this experience has led me to make further enquiries into the nature of happenings of this kind, with the result, that after carefully eliminating all cases which could be accounted for in any other manner, I have found myself compelled to admit a considerable number of instances of what are called "ghosts," on the word of persons whose veracity and soundness of judgment I should not doubt on any other subject. It is often said that you never meet any one who has himself seen a ghost, but only those who have heard of somebody else seeing one. This I can entirely contradict, for I have met with many trustworthy persons of both sexes, who have given me accounts of such appearances having been actually witnessed by themselves. In conclusion, I may mention that I was telling this story some twenty years later to a Colonel Fox, who had known the unfortunate man who committed suicide, and he said to me: "Do you know what were the last words he said to his wife?"

"No," I replied.

"The very same words he spoke to your wife," said Colonel Fox.

This is the story I refer to in my book "Bible Mystery and Bible Meaning" as that of "the Ghost that I did not see." I do not attempt to offer any explanation of it, but merely give the facts as they occurred, and the reader must form his own theory on the subject; but the reason I bring in this story in the present connection is, that in this instance there could be no question of the physical body contributing to the psychic phenomenon, since the person seen had been dead for nearly twenty years; and coupling this fact with the distance from the physical body at which the psychic action took place in the other cases I have mentioned, I think there is a very strong presumption that the psychic powers can, and do, act independently of the physical body; though of course it does not follow from this that they cannot also act in conjunction with it.

On the other hand, a comparison of the present case with those previously mentioned, fails to throw any light on the important question whether the deceased feels any consciousness of the action which the percipient sees, or whether what is seen is like a sort of photograph impressed upon the atmosphere of a particular locality, and visible only to certain persons, who are able to sense etheric wave-lengths which are outside the range of the single octave forming the solar spectrum. It throws no light on this question, because, in the case of my being seen by Mr. S. in Edinburgh and that of Miss B. and her mother being seen by me at Norwood, none of us were conscious of having been at those places; while in the case of my psychic visit to Lanercost Abbey, and other similar experiences I have had, I have been fully aware of seeing the places in question. The evidence tells both ways, and I can therefore only infer that there are two modes of psychic action, in one of which the person projecting that action, whether voluntarily or involuntarily, experiences corresponding sensations, and the other in which he does not; but I am unable to offer any criterion by which the observer can, with certainty, distinguish between the two.

It appears to me, that such instances as those I have mentioned, point to ranges of etheric action beyond those ordinarily recognized by physical science, but the principle seems to be the same, and it is for this reason that I have taken the modern scientific theory of etheric vibration as our starting-point. The universe is one great whole, and the laws of one part cannot contradict those of another; therefore the explanation of such queer happenings is not to be found by denying the well-ascertained laws of Nature on the physical plane, but by considering whether these laws do not extend further. It is on this account that I would lay stress on the Mathematical side of things, and have adduced instances where various discoveries have been made by following up the sequence indicated by the laws already known, and which have thus enabled us to fill up gaps in our knowledge, which would otherwise stop, or at least seriously hinder, our further progress. It is in this way that Jachin helps Boaz, and that the undeviating nature of Law, so far from limiting us, becomes our faithful ally if we will only allow it to do so.

I think, then, that the scientific idea of the ether, as a universal medium pervading all space, and permeating all substance, will help us to see that many things which are popularly called supernatural, are to be attributed to the action of known laws working under, as yet, unknown conditions, and therefore, when we are confronted with strange phenomena, a knowledge of the general principles involved, will show us in what direction to look for an explanation. Now applying this to the present subject, we may reasonably argue, that since all physical matter is scientifically proved to consist of the universal ether in various degrees of condensation, there may be other degrees of condensation, forming other modes of matter, which are beyond the scope of physical vision and of our laboratory apparatus. And similarly, we may argue, that just as various effects can be produced on the physical plane, by the action of etheric waves of various lengths, so other effects might be produced on these finer modes of matter, by etheric waves of other lengths. And in this connection we must not forget that a gap occurs between the "dark heat" groups and the Hertzian group, consisting of five octaves of waves, the lengths of which have been theoretically calculated, but whose action has not yet been discovered. Here we admittedly have a wide field for the working of known laws under as yet unknown conditions; and again, how can we say that there are not ranges of unknown waves, yet smaller than the minute ultra-violet ones, which commence the present known scale, or transcending those largest ones, which bear our messages across the Atlantic? Mathematically, there is no limit to the scale in either direction; and so, taking our stand on the demonstrated facts of science, we find, that the known laws of Nature point to their continuation in modes of matter and of force, of which we have as yet no conception. It is therefore not at all necessary to spurn the ground of established science to spread the wings of our fancy; rather it affords us the requisite basis from which to start, just as the aeronaut cannot rise without a solid surface from which to spring.

Now if we realize that the ether is an infinitely subtle fluid, pervading all space, we see that it must constitute a connecting link between all modes of substance, whether visible or invisible, in all worlds, and may therefore be called the Universal Medium; and following up our conception of the Continuity of Law, we may suppose that trains of waves, inconceivably smaller or greater than any known to modern science, are set up in this medium, in the same way as the electro-magnetic waves with which we are acquainted; that is, by an impulse which generates them from some particular point. In the region of finer forces we are now prospecting, this impulse might well be the Desire or Will of the spiritual entity which we ourselves are—that thinking, feeling, inmost essence of ourself, which is the "noumenon" of our individuality, and which, for the sake of brevity we call our "Ego," a Latin word which simply means "I myself." This idea of spiritual impulse is quite familiar to us in our every-day talk. We speak of an impulsive person, meaning one who acts on a sudden thought without giving due heed to consequences; so in our ordinary speech we look upon thought as the initial impulse, only we restrict this to the case of unregulated thought. But if unregulated thought acts as a centre of impulse, why should not regulated thought do the same? Therefore we may accept the idea of Thought as the initial impulse, which starts trains of waves in the Universal Medium, whether with or without due consideration, and having thus recognized its dynamic power, we must learn to make the impulsions we thus send forth intelligent, well defined, and directed to some useful purpose. The operator at some wireless station does not use his instruments to send out a lot of jumbled-up waves into the ether, but controls the impulsions into a definite and intelligible order, and we must do the same.

On some such lines as these, then, we may picture the desire of the Ego as starting a train of waves in the Universal Medium, which are reproduced in corresponding *form* on reaching their destination. As with the electro-magnetic waves, they may spread all round, just as ripples do if we throw a stone into a pond; but they will only take form where there is a correspondence able to receive them. This is what in the language of electrical engineers is called "Syntony," which means being tuned to the same rate of vibration, and no doubt it is from some such cause, that we sometimes experience what seem inexplicable feelings of attraction or repulsion towards different persons. This also appears to furnish a key to thought-transference, hypnotism, and other allied phenomena.

If the reader questions whether thought is capable of generating impulses in the etheric medium I would refer him to the experiment mentioned in Chapter XIV of my "Edinburgh Lectures on Mental Science," where I describe how, when operating with Dr. Baraduc's biometer, I found that the needle revolved through a smaller or large arc of the circle, in response to my mental intention of concentrating a smaller or larger degree of force upon it. Perhaps you will say that the difference in the movement of the needle depended on the quantity of magnetism that was flowing from me, to say nothing of other known forces, such as heat, light, electricity, etc. Well, that is precisely the proposition I am putting forward. What caused the difference in the intensity of the magnetic flow was my intention of varying it, so that we come back to mental action as the centre of impulsion from which the etheric waves were generated. If, then, such a demonstration can be obtained on the plane of purely physical matter, why need we doubt that the same Law will work in the same way, in respect of those finer modes of substance, and wider ranges of etheric vibrations, which, starting from the basis of recognized physical science, the Law of Continuity would lead to by an orderly sequence, and which the occurrence of what, for want of a better name, we call occult phenomena require for their explanation?

Before passing on to the more practical generalizations to be drawn from the suggestions contained in this chapter, I may advert to an objection sometimes brought by the sceptical in this matter. They say: "How is it that apparitions are always seen in the dark?" and then they answer their own question by saying, it is because superstitious people are nervous in the dark and imagine all sorts of things. Then they laugh and think they have disposed of the whole subject. But it is not disposed of quite so easily, for not only are there many well attested cases of such appearances in broad daylight, but there are also scientific facts, showing that if we are right in explaining such happenings by etheric action, such action is more readily produced at night than in the presence of sunlight.

In the early part of 1902 Marconi made some experiments on board the American liner *Philadelphia,* which brought out the remarkable fact that, while it was possible to transmit signals to a distance of fifteen hundred miles during the night, they could not be transmitted further than seven hundred miles during the day. The same was found to be the case by Lieutenant Solari of the Italian Navy, at whose disposal the ship *Carlo Alberta* was placed by the King of Italy in 1902, for the purpose of making investigations into wireless telegraphy; and summing up the points which he considered to have been fully established by his experiments on board that ship, he mentions among them the fact, that sunlight has the effect of reducing the power of the electro-magnetic waves, and that consequently a greater force is required to produce a given result by day than by night. Here, then, is a reason why we might expect to see more supernatural appearances, as we call them, at night than in the day—they require a smaller amount of force to produce them. At the same time, it is found that the great magnetic waves which cover immense distances, work even more powerfully in the light than in the dark. May it not be that these things show, that there is more than a merely metaphorical use of words, when the Bible tells us of the power of Light to dissipate, and bring to naught, the powers of Darkness, while the Light itself is the Great Power, using the forces of the universe on the widest scale? Perhaps it is none other than the continuity of unchanging universal principles extending into the mysterious realms of the spiritual world.

CHAPTER III

MAN'S PLACE IN THE CREATIVE ORDER

In the preceding chapters we have found certain definite facts,—that all known matter is formed out of one primordial Universal Substance,—that the ether spreading throughout limitless space is a Universal Medium, through which it is possible to convey force by means of vibrations,—and that vibrations can be started by the power of Sound. These we have found to be well established facts of ordinary science, and taking them as our starting-point, we may now begin to speculate as to the possible workings of the known laws under unknown conditions.

One of the first things that naturally attract our attention is the question,—How did Life originate? On this point I may quote two leading men of science. Tyndall says: "I affirm that no shred of trustworthy experimental testimony exists, to prove that life in our day has ever appeared independently of antecedent life"; and Huxley says: "The doctrine of biogenesis, or life only from life, is victorious along the whole line at the present time." Such is the testimony of modern science to the old maxim "Omne vivum exvivo." "All life proceeds from antecedent life." Think it out for yourself and you will see that it could not possibly be otherwise.

Whatever may be our theory of the origin of life on the physical plane, whether we regard it as commencing in a vivified slime at the bottom of the sea, which we call protoplasm, or in any other way, the question of how life got there still remains unanswered. The protoplasm being material substance, must have its origin like all other material substances, in the undifferentiated etheric Universal Substance, no particle of which has any power of operating upon any other particle until some initial vibration starts the movement; so that, on any theory whatever, we are always brought back to the same question: What started the condensation of the ether into the beginnings of a world-system? So whether we consider the life which characterizes organized matter, or the energy which characterizes inorganic matter, we cannot avoid the conclusion, that both must have their source in some Original Power to which we can assign no antecedent. This is the conclusion which has been reached by all philosophic and religious systems that have really tried to get at the root of the matter, simply because it is impossible to form any other conception.

This Living Power is what we mean when we speak of the All-Originating Spirit. The existence of this Spirit is not a theological invention, but a logical and scientific ultimate, without predicating which, nothing else can be accounted for. The word "Spirit" comes from the Latin "spiro" "I breathe," and so means "The Breath," as in Job xxxiii, 4,—"The Spirit of God hath made me, and the breath of the Almighty hath given me life"; and again in Ps. xxxiii, 6—"By the word of the Lord were the heavens made, and all the host of them by the breath of his mouth."

In the opening chapter of Genesis, we are told that "the Spirit of God moved upon the face of the waters." The words rendered "the Spirit of God" are, in the original Hebrew "rouah Ælohim," which is literally "the Breathing of God"; and similarly, the ancient religious books of India, make the "Swára" or Great Breath the commencement of all life and energy. The word "rouah" in Genesis is remarkable. According to rabbinical teaching, each letter of the Hebrew alphabet has a certain symbolic significance, and when examined in this manner, the root from which this word is derived conveys the idea of Expansive Movement. It is the opposite of the word "hoshech," translated "darkness" in the same passage of our Bible, which is similarly derived from a root conveying the idea of Hardening and Compressing. It is the same idea that is personified in the Zendavesta, the sacred book of the ancient Persians, under the names of Ormuzd, the Spirit of Light; and Ahriman, the Spirit of Darkness; and similarly in the old Assyrian myth of the struggle between the Sun-God and Tiámat, the goddess of darkness.

This conception of conflict between two opposite principles, Light and Darkness, Compression and Expansion, will be found to underlie all the ancient religions of the world, and it is conspicuous throughout our own Scriptures. But it should be borne in mind that the oppositeness of their nature does not necessarily mean conflict. The two principles of Expansion and Contraction are not necessarily destructive; on the contrary they are necessary correlatives to one another. Expansion alone cannot produce form; cohesion must also be present. It is the regulated balance between them that results in Creation. In the old legend, if I remember rightly, the conflict is ended by Tiámat marrying her former opponent. They were never really enemies, but there was a misunderstanding between them, or rather there was a misunderstanding on the part of Tiámat so long as she did not perceive the true character of the Spirit of Light, and that their relation to one another was that of co-operation and not of opposition. Thus also St. John tells us that "the light shineth in darkness and the darkness comprehended it not" (John i, 5). It is this want of comprehension that is at the root of all the trouble.

The reader should note, however, that I am here speaking of that Primeval Substance, which necessarily has no light in itself, because there is as yet no vibration in it, for there can be no light without vibration. We must not make the mistake of supposing that Matter is evil in itself: it is our misconception of it that makes it the vehicle of evil; and we must distinguish between the darkness of Matter and moral darkness, though there is a spiritual correspondence between them. The true development of Man consists in the self-expansion of the Divine Spirit working through his mind, and thence upon his psychic and physical organisms, but this can only be by the individual's *willingness to receive* that Spirit. Where the hindrance to this working is only caused by ignorance of the true relation between ourselves and the Divine Spirit, and the desire for truth is present, the True Light will in due course disperse the darkness. But on the other hand, if the hindrance is caused by *unwillingness* to be led by the Divine Spirit, then the Light cannot be *forced* upon any one, and for this reason Jesus said: "This is the condemnation, that light is come into the World, and men loved darkness rather than light, because their deeds were evil. For every one that doeth evil hateth the light, neither cometh to the light, lest his deeds should be reproved. But he that doeth truth cometh to the light, that his deeds may be made manifest, that they are wrought in God" (John iii: 19-21). In physical science these things have an exact parallel in "Ohm's Law" regarding the resistance offered by the conductor to the flow of the electric current. The correspondence is very remarkable and will be found more fully explained in a later chapter. The Primary Darkness, both of Substance and of Mind, has to be taken into account, if we would form an intelligent conception of the twofold process of Involution and Evolution continually at work in ourselves, which, by their combined action, are able to lead to the limitless development both of the individual and of the race.

According to all teaching, then, both ancient and modern, all life and energy have their source in a Primary Life and Energy, of which we can only say that IT IS. We cannot conceive of any time when it was not, for, if there was a time when no such Primary Energizing Life existed, what was there to energize it? So we are landed in a *reductio ad absurdum* which leaves no alternative but to predicate the Eternal Existence of an All-Originating Living Spirit.

Let us stop for a moment to consider what we mean by "Eternal." When, do you suppose, twice two began to make four? And when, do you suppose, twice two will cease to make four? It is an eternal principle, quite independent of time or conditions. Similarly with the Originating Life. It is above time and above conditions—in a word it is *undifferentiated* and contains in itself the *potential* of infinite differentiation. This is what the Eternal Life is, and what we want for the expansion of our own life is a truer comprehension of it. We are like Tiámat, and must enter into intelligent and loving union with the Spirit of Light, in order to realize the infinite possibilities that lie before us. This is the ultimate meaning of the maxim "Omne vivum ex vivo."

We see, then, that the material universe, including our own bodies, has its origin in the undifferentiated Universal Substance, and that the first movement towards differentiation must be started by some initial impulse, analogous to those which start vibrations in the ether known to science; and that therefore this impulse must, in the first instance, proceed from some Living Power eternal in itself, and independent of time and conditions. Now all the ancient religions of the world concur, in attributing this initial impulse to the power of Sound; and we have seen, that as a matter of fact, sound has the power of starting vibrations, and that these vibrations have an exact correspondence with the quality of the sound, what we now call synchronous vibration.

At this point, however, we are met by another fact. Cosmic activity takes place only in certain definite areas. Solar systems do not jostle each other in space. In a word the Sound, which thus starts the initial impulse of creation, is guided by Intelligent Selection. Now sounds, directed by purposeful intention, amount to Words, whether the words of some spoken language or the tapping of the Morse code—it is the meaning at the back of the sound that gives it verbal significance. It is for this reason, that the concentration of creative energy in particular areas, has from time immemorial been attributed to "The Word." The old Sanskrit books call this selective concentrative power "Vach," which means "Voice," and is the root of the Latin word "Vox," having the same meaning. Philo, and the Neo-Platonists of Alexandria who follow him, call it "Logos," which means the same; and we are all familiar with the opening verses of St. John's Gospel and First Epistle in which he attributes Creation to "The Word."

Now we know, as a scientific fact, that solar systems have a definite beginning in the gyration of nebulous matter, circling through vast fields of interstellar space, as the great nebula in Andromeda does at the present day. Æons upon æons elapse, before the primary nebula consolidates into a solar system such as ours is now; but science shows, that from the time when the nebula first spreads its spiral across the heavens, the mathematical element of Law asserts itself, and it is by means of our recognition of the mathematical relations between the forces of attraction and repulsion, that we have been able to acquire any knowledge on the subject. I do not for an instant wish to suggest that the Spiritual Power has not continued to be in operation also, but a centre for the working of a Cosmic Law being once established, the Spiritual Power works through that Law and not in opposition to it. On the other hand, the selection of particular portions of space for the manifestation of cosmic activity, indicates the action of free volition, not determined by any law except the obvious consideration of allowing room for the future solar system to move in. Similarly also with regard to time. Spectroscopic analysis of the light from the stars, which are suns many of them much greater than our own, shows that they are of various ages—some quite young, some arrived at maturity, and some passing into old age. Their creation must therefore be assigned to different epochs, and we thus see the Originating Spirit exercising the powers of Selection and Volition as to the time when, as well as to the place where, a new world-system shall be inaugurated.

Now it is this power of inauguration that all the ancient systems of teaching attribute to the Divine Word. It is the passing of the undifferentiated into differentiation, of the unmanifested into manifestation, of the unlocalized into localization. It is the ushering in of what the Brahminical books call a "Manvantara" or world-period, and in like manner our Bible says that "In the beginning was the Word." The English word "word" is closely allied to the Latin word "verbum" which signifies both *word* and *verb*. Grammarians tell us that the verb "to be" is a verb-substantive, that is, it does not indicate any action passing from the subject to the object. Now this exactly describes the Spirit in its Eternity. We cannot conceive of It except as always BEING; but the distribution of world-systems both in time and space shows that it is not always cosmically active. In itself, apart from manifestation, it is Pure Beingness, if I may coin such a word; and it is for this reason that the Divine Name announced to Moses was "I AM." But the fact that Creation exists, shows that from this Substantive Pure Being there flows out a Verb Active, which reproduces in action, what the I AM is in essence. It is just the same with ourselves. We must first *be* before we can *do*, and we can *do* only to the extent to which we *are*. We cannot express powers which we do not possess; so that our doing necessarily coincides with the quality of our being. Therefore the Divine Verb reproduces the Divine Substantive by a natural sequence. It is *generated* by the Divine "I AM," and for this reason it is called "The Son of God." So we see that The Verb, The Word, and The Son of God, are all different expressions for the same Power.

Creative vibration in the Universal Substance can, therefore, only be conceived of, as being inaugurated by the "Word" which *localizes* the activity of the Spirit in particular centres. This idea, of the localization of the Spirit through the "Word," should be fully realized as the energizing principle on the scale of the Macrocosm or "Great World," because, as we shall find later on, the same principle acts in the same way on the scale of the Microcosm or "Small World," which is the individual man. This is why these things have a personal interest for us, otherwise they would not be worth troubling about. But a mistake to be avoided at this point, is that of supposing that the "Word" is something which dictates to the Spirit when and where to operate. The "Word" is the word of the Spirit itself, and not that of some higher authority, for the Spirit being First Cause there can be nothing anterior to dictate to it; there can be nothing before that which is First. The "Word" which centralizes the activity of the Spirit, is therefore that of the Spirit itself. We have an analogy in our own case. If I go to New York the first movement in that direction is that of my Thought or Desire. It is true that in my present state of evolution I have to follow the usual methods of travel, but so far as my Thought is concerned, I have been there all the time. Indeed, such a case as the one I have mentioned, of my being seen in Edinburgh while I was physically in London, seems to point to the actual transference of some part of the personality to another locality, and similarly with my visit to Lanercost Abbey; and the reader must remember, that such phenomena are by no means uncommon—they are the natural action of some part of our personality, and must therefore follow some natural law, even though we may at present know very little of how it works.

We see, therefore, both from *a priori* reasoning, and from observed facts, that it is the Word, Thought, or Desire of the Spirit, that localizes its activity in some definite centre. The student should bear this in mind as a leading principle, for he will find that it is of general application, alike in the case of individuals, of groups of individuals, and of entire nations. It is the key to the relation between Law and Personality, the opening of the Grand Arcanum, the equilibrating of Jachin and Boaz, and it is therefore of immediate importance to ourselves.

We may take, then, as a starting-point for further enquiry, the maxim that Volition creates Centres of Spiritual Activity. But perhaps you will say: "If this be true, what word or words am I to employ?" This is a question which has puzzled a good many people before you. This "Word" which so many have been in search of, has been variously called "the Lost Word," "the Word of Power," "the Schemhammaphorasch or Secret Name of God," and so on. A quaint Jewish legend of the Middle Ages says that the "Hidden Name" was secretly inscribed in the innermost recesses of the Temple; but that, even if discovered, which was most unlikely, it could not be retained because, guarding it, were sculptured lions, which gave such a supernatural roar as the intruder was quitting the spot, that all memory of the "Hidden Name" was driven from his mind. Jesus, however, says the legend, knew this and dodged the lions. He transcribed the Name, and cutting open his thigh, hid the writing in the incision, which, by magical art, he at once closed up; then, after leaving the Temple, he took the writing out and so retained the knowledge of the Name. In this way the legend accounts for his power to work miracles.

Jesus, indeed, possessed the Word of Power, though not in the way told in the legend, and he repeatedly proclaimed it in his teaching:—"According to your Faith be it unto you"—"Verily, I say unto you, whosoever shall say to this mountain, 'Be thou taken up and cast into the sea'; and shall not doubt in his heart, but shall believe that what he saith shall come to pass, he shall have whatsoever he saith" (Mark xi, 23). And similarly in the Old Testament we are told that the Word is nigh to us, even in our hearts and in our mouth (Deut. xxx, 14). What keeps the Word of Power hidden, is our belief that nothing so simple could possibly be it.

At the same time, simple though it be, it has Law and Reason at the back of it, like everything else. The ancient Egyptians seem to have had clearer ideas on this subject than we have. "The name was to the Egyptians the *idea* of the thing, without which it could not exist, and the knowledge of which therefore gave power over that which answered to it." "The *idea* of the thing represented its *soul*." [2] This is the same conception as the "archetypal ideas" of Plato, only carried further, so as to apply, not only to classes, but to each individual of the class, and, as we shall see later, there is a good deal of truth in it. Put broadly, the conception is this—every external fact must have a spiritual origin, an internal energizing principle, which causes it to exist in the particular form in which it does. The outward fact is called the Phenomenon, and the corresponding inward principle is called the Noumenon. The dictionary definition of these two words is as follows: "Phenomenon—the appearance which anything makes to our consciousness as distinguished from what it is in itself." "Noumenon—an unknown and unknowable substance or thing as it is in itself—the opposite to the Phenomenon or form through which it becomes known to the senses or the understanding" (Chambers' Twentieth Century Dictionary). Whether the dictionary be right in saying that the "noumena" of things are entirely unknowable, the reader must decide for himself; but the present book is an attempt to learn something about the "noumena" of things in general, and of ourselves in particular, and what I want to convey is, that the "noumenon" of anything is its essence, *in terms of the Universal Energy and the Universal Substance, in their relation to the particular Form in question*. Probably the Latin word "Nomen," a Name, is derived from this Greek word, and in this sense everything has its "hidden name"; and the region in which Thought-Power works, is this region of spiritual beginnings. It deals with "hidden names"—that inward essence which determines the outward form of things, persons, and circumstances alike; and it is in order to make this clearer, that I have commenced by sketching briefly the general principles of Substance and Energy as now recognized by modern science.

If I have made my meaning clear, you will see that what is wanted is not the knowledge of particular words, but an understanding of general principles. At the same time I would not assert that the reciting of certain forms of words, such as the Indian "mantras" or the word AUM, to which Oriental teachers attach a mystic significance, is entirely without power. But the power is not in the words *but in our belief in their power*. I will give an amusing instance of this. On several occasions I have been consulted by persons who supposed themselves to be under the influence of "malicious magnetism," emanating in some cases from known, and in others from unknown, sources; and the remedy I have prescribed has been this. Look the adverse power, mentally, full in the face, and then assuming an attitude of confidence say "Cock-a-doodle-doo." The enquirers have sometimes smiled at first, but in every case the result has been successful. Perhaps this is why Æsculapius is represented as accompanied by a cock. Possibly the ancient physicians were in the habit of employing the "Cock-a-doodle-doo" treatment; and I might recommend it to the faculty to-day as very effective in certain cases. Now I do not think the reader will attribute any particularly occult significance to "Cock-a-doodle-doo." The power is in the mental attitude. To "cock-a-doodle-doo" at any suggestion is to treat it with scorn and derision, and to assume the very opposite of that receptive attitude which enables a suggestion to affect us. That is the secret of this method of treatment, and the principle is the same in all cases.

It matters, then, very little what particular words we use. What does matter is the intention and faith with which we use them. But perhaps some reader will here take the rôle of cross-examining counsel, and say: "You have just said it is a case of synchronous vibration—then surely it is the actual sound of the particular syllables that counts—how do you square this with your present statement?" The answer is that the Law is always the same, but the mode of response to the Law is always according to the nature of the medium in which it is operating. On the plane of physical matter the vibrations are in tune with physical sounds, as in the experiments with the eidophone; and similarly, on the plane of ideas or "noumena," the response is in terms of that plane. The word which creates "noumena," or spiritual centres of action, must itself belong to the world of "noumena," so that it is not illogical to say that it is the intention and faith that counts, and not the external sound. In this is the secret of the Power of Thought. It is the reproduction, on the miniature scale of the individual, of the same mode of Power that makes the worlds. It is that Power of Personality, which, combined with the action of the Law, brings out results which the Law alone could never do—as the old maxim has it, "Nature unaided fails."

This brings us to another important question—is not the creative power of the Word limited by the immutability of the Law? If the Law cannot be altered in the least particular, how can the Word be free to do what it likes? The answer to this is contained in another maxim: "Every creation carries its own mathematics along with it." You cannot create anything without at the same time creating its relation to everything else, just as in painting a landscape, the contour you give to the trees will determine that of the sky. Therefore, whenever you create anything, you thereby start a train of causation, which will work out in strict accordance with the sort of thought that started it. The stream always has the quality of its source. Thought which is in line with the Unity of the Great Whole, will produce correspondingly harmonious results, and Thought which is disruptive of the great Principle of Unity, will produce correspondingly disputive results—hence all the trouble and confusion in the world. Our Thought is perfectly free, and we can use it either constructively or destructively as we choose; but the immutable Law of Sequence will not permit us to plant a thought of one kind, and make it bear fruit of another.

Then the question very naturally suggests itself: Why did not God create us so that we could not think negative or destructive thoughts? And the answer is: Because He could not. There are some things which even God cannot do. He cannot do anything that involves a contradiction in terms. Even God could not make twice two either more or less than four. Now I want the student to see clearly why making us incapable of wrong-thinking would involve a contradiction in terms, and would therefore be an impossibility. To see this we must realize what is our place in the Order of the Universe. The name "Man" itself indicates this. It comes from the Sanscrit root MN, which, in all its derivatives, conveys the idea of Measurement, as in the word Mind, through the Latin *mens,* the faculty which compares things and estimates them accordingly; Moon, the heavenly body whose phases afford the most obvious standard for the periodical measurement of time; Month, the period thus measured; "Man," the largest of the Indian weights; and so on. Man therefore means "The Measurer," and this very aptly describes our place in the order of evolution, for it indicates the relation between Personal Volition and Immutable Law.

If we grant the truth of the maxim "Nature unaided fails" the whole thing becomes clear, and the entire progress of applied science proves the truth of this maxim. To recur to an illustration I have employed in my previous books, the old ship-builders thought that ships were bound to be built of wood and not of iron, because wood floats in water and iron sinks; but now nearly all ships are made of iron. Yet the specific gravities of wood and iron have not altered, and a log of wood floats while a lump of iron sinks, just the same as they did in the days of Drake and Frobisher. The only difference is, that people thought out the *underlying principle* of the law of flotation, and reduced it to the generalized statement that anything will float, the weight of which is less than that of the mass displaced by it, whether it be an iron ship floating in water, or a balloon floating in air. So long as we restrict ourselves to the mere recollection of observed facts, we shall make no progress; but by carefully considering *why* any force acted in the way it did, under the particular conditions observed, we arrive at a generalization of principle, showing that the force in question is capable of hitherto unexpected applications if we provide the necessary conditions. This is the way in which all advances have been made on the material side, and on the principle of Continuity we may reasonably infer that the same applies to the spiritual side also.

We may generalize the whole position thus. When we first observe the working of the Law under the conditions spontaneously provided by Nature, it appears to limit us; but by seeking the *reason* of the action exhibited under these limited conditions, we discover the principle, and true nature, of the Law in question, and we then learn from the Law itself, what conditions to supply in order to give it more extended scope, and direct its energy to the accomplishment of definite purposes. The maxim we have to learn is that "Every Law *contains in itself* the principle of its own Expansion," which will set us free from the limitation which that Law at first appeared to impose upon us. The limitation was never in the Law, but in the conditions under which it was working, and our power of selection and volition enables us to provide new conditions, not spontaneously provided by Nature, and thus to *specialize* the Law, and disclose immense powers which had always been latent in it, but which would for ever remain hidden unless brought to light by the co-operation of the Personal Factor. The Law itself never changes, but we can *specialize* it by realizing the principle involved and providing the conditions thus indicated. This is our place in the Order of the Universe. We give definite direction to the action of the Law, and in this way our Personal Factor is always acting upon the law, whether we know it or not; and the Law, under the influence thus impressed upon it, is all the time re-acting upon us.

Now we cannot conceive any limit to Evolution. To suppose a point where it comes to an end is a contradiction in terms. It is to suppose that the Eternal Life Principle is used up, which is to deny its Eternity; and, as we have seen, unless we assume its Eternity, it is impossible to account either for our own existence or that of anything else. Therefore, to say that a point will ever be reached where it will be used up, is as absurd as saying that a point will be reached where the sequence of numbers will be used up. Evolution, the progress from lower to higher modes of manifestation of the underlying Principle of Life, is therefore eternal, but, in regard to the human race, this progress depends entirely on the extent to which we grasp the principles of the Law of our own Being, and so learn to specialize it in the right direction. Then if this be our place in the Universal Order, it becomes clear that we could not occupy this place unless we had a perfectly free hand to choose the conditions under which the Law is to operate; and therefore, in order to pass beyond the limits of the mineral, vegetable and animal kingdoms, and reach the status of being Persons, and not things, we must have a freedom of selection and volition, which makes it equally possible for us to select either rightly or wrongly; and the purpose of sound teaching is to make us see the eternal principles involved, and thus lead us to impress our Personality upon the Law, in the way that will bring out the infinite possibilities of good which the Law, rightly employed, contains. If it were possible to do this by an automatic Law, doubtless the Creative Wisdom would have made us so. This is why St. Paul says: "If there had been a law given which could have given life, verily righteousness should have been by the law" (Gal. iii, 21). Note the words "a law *given*," that is to say, imposed by external command; but it could not be. The laws of the Universe are Cosmic. In themselves they are *impersonal*, and the infinite possibilities contained in them, can only be brought out by the co-operation of the Personal Factor. It is only as we grasp the true relation between Jachin and Boaz, that we can enter into the Temple either of our own Individuality, or of the boundless Universe in which we live. The reason, therefore, why God did not make us mechanically incapable of wrong thinking, is simply because the very idea involves a contradiction in terms, which negatives all possibility of Creation. The conception lands us in a *reductio ad absurdum*.

Therefore, we are free to use our powers of Personality as we will, only we must take the consequences. Now one error we are all very apt to fall into, is the mistaken use of the Will. Its proper function is to keep our other faculties in line with the Law, and thus enable us to specialize it; but many people seem to think that by force of will they can somehow manage to coerce the Law; in other words, that by force of will they can sow a seed of one kind and make it bear fruit of another. The Spirit of Life seeks to express itself in our individuality, through the three avenues of reason, feeling, and will; but as in the Masonic legend of the murder of Hiram Abif, the architect of Solomon's Temple, it is beaten back on the side of reasoning, by the plummet of a logic based on false premises; on the side of feeling, by the level of conventional ideas; and on the side of will, by the hammer of a short-sighted self-will, which gives the finishing blow; and it is not until the true perception of the Principle of Life is resurrected within us, that the Temple can be completed according to the true plan.

It should be remembered that the will is *not* the Creative Faculty in us. It is the faculty of Conception that is the creative agent, and the business of the Will is to keep that faculty in the right direction, which will be determined by an enlightened Reason. Conception creates ideas which are the seed, that, in due time, will produce fruit after its own kind. In a broad sense we may call it the Imaging Faculty, only we must not suppose that this necessarily implies the visualizing of mental images, which is only a subsidiary mode of using this faculty. An "immaculate conception" is therefore the only means by which the New Liberated Man can be born in each of us. The sequence is always the same. The Will holds the Conception together, and the idea thus formed gives direction to the working of the Law. But this direction may be either true or inverted; and the impersonal Law will work constructively or destructively, according to the conception which it embodies. In this way, then, willpower may be used to hold together an inverted conception—the conception that our personal force of will is sufficient to bear down all opposition. But this mental attitude ignores the fact, that the fundamental principle of creative power is the Wholeness of the Creation; and that, therefore, the idea of forcing compliance with our wishes, by the power of our individual will, is an inverted conception, which, though it may appear to succeed for a time, is bound to fail eventually, because it antagonizes the very power it is seeking to use. This inverted use of the Will is the basis of "Black Magic," a term some readers will perhaps smile at, but which is practised at the present day to a much greater extent than many of us have any idea of—not always, indeed, with a full consciousness of its nature, but in many ways which are the first steps on the Left-hand Path. Its mark is the determination to act by Self-will, rather than using our will to co-operate with that continuous forward movement of the Great Whole, which is the Will of God. This inverted will entirely misses the point regarding the part we are formed to play in the Creative Order, and so we miss the development of our own individuality, and retrograde instead of going forward.

But if we work *with* the Law instead of against it, we shall find that our word, that is to say our conception, will become more and more the Word of Power, because it specializes the general Law in some particular direction. The Law will serve us exactly to the extent to which we first observe the Law. It is the same in everything. If the electrician tries to go counter to the fundamental principle, that the electric current always flows from a higher to a lower potential, he will be able to do nothing with it; but let him observe this fundamental law and there is nothing that electricity will not do for him within the field of its own nature. In this sense, then, of specializing the general Law in a particular direction, we may lay down the maxim that "The Law flows from the Word, and not *vice versa*."

When we use our Word in this way, not as expressing a self-will that seeks to crush all that does not submit to it, but as a portion, however small, of the Universal Cause, and therefore with the desire of acting in harmony with that Cause, then our word becomes a constructive, instead of a destructive power. Its influence may be very small at first, because there is still a great mass of doubt at the back of our mind, and every doubt is, in reality, a Negative Word warring against our Affirmative Word; but, by adhering to our principle, we shall gradually gain experience in these things, and the creative value of our word will grow accordingly.

CHAPTER IV

THE LAW OF WHOLENESS

It may seem a truism to say that the whole is made up of its parts, but all the same we often lose sight of this in our outlook on life.

The reason we do so is because we are apt to take too narrow a view of the whole; and also because we do not sufficiently consider that it is not the mere arithmetical sum of the parts that makes the whole, but also the harmonious agreement of each part with all the other parts. The extent of the whole and the harmony of the parts is what we have to look out for, and also its objective; this is a universal rule, whatever the whole in question may be.

Take, for instance, the case of the artist. He must start by having a definite objective, what in studio phrase is called a "motif"; something that has given him a certain impression which he wants to convey to others, but which cannot be stated as an isolated fact without any surroundings. Then the surroundings must be painted so as to have a natural relation to the main motif; they must lead up to it, but at the same time they must not compete with it. There must be only one definite interest in the picture, and minor details must not be allowed to interfere with it. They are there only because of the main motif, to help to express it. Yet they are not to be treated in a slovenly manner. As much as is seen of them must be drawn with an accuracy that correctly suggests their individual character; but they must not be accentuated in such a way as to emphasize details to the detriment of the breadth of the picture. This is the artistic principle of unity, and the same principle applies to everything else.

What, then, is the "Motif" of Life? Surely it must be, to express its own Livingness. Then in the True Order all modes of life and energy must converge towards this end, and it is only our short-sightedness that prevents us from seeing this,—from seeing that the greater the harmony of the whole Life, the greater will be the inflow of that Life in each of the parts that are giving it expression. This is what we want to learn with regard to ourselves, whether as individuals, classes or nations. We have seen the cosmic workings of the Law of Wholeness in the discovery of the planet Neptune. Another planet was absolutely necessary to complete the unity of our solar system, and it was found that there is such a planet, and similarly in other branches of natural science. The Law of Unity is the basic law of Life, and it is our ignorant or wilful infraction of this Law that is the root of all our troubles.

If we take this Law of Unity as the basis of our Thought we shall be surprised to find how far it will carry us. Each part is a complete whole in itself. Each inconceivably minute particle revolves round the centre of the atom in its own orbit. On its own scale it is complete in itself, and by co-operation with thousands of others forms the atom. The atom again is a complete whole, but it must combine with other atoms to form a molecule, and so on. But if the atom be imperfect as an atom, how could it combine with other atoms?

Thus we see that however infinitesimal any part may be as compared with the whole, it must also be a complete whole on its own scale, if the greater whole is to be built up. On the same principle, our recognition that our personality is an infinitesimal fraction of an inconceivably greater Life, does not mean that it is at all insignificant in itself, or that our individuality becomes submerged in an indistinguishable mass; on the contrary, our own wholeness is an essential factor towards the building up of the greater whole; so that as long as we keep before us the building up of the Great Whole as the "main motif," we need never fear the expansion of our own individuality. The more we expand, the more effective units we shall become.

We must not, however, suppose that Unity means Uniformity. St. Paul puts this very clearly when he says, if the whole body be an eye, where would be the hearing, etc. (1 Cor. xii, 14). How could you paint a picture without distinction of form, colour, or tone? Diversity in Unity is the necessity for any sort of expression, and if it be the case in our own bodies, as St. Paul points out, how much more so in the expressing of the Eternal Life through endless ages and limitless space! Once we grasp this idea of the unity and progressiveness of Life going on *ad infinitum*, what boundless vistas of possibility open before us. It would be enough to stagger the imagination were it not for our old friends, the Law and the Word. But these will always accompany us, and we may rely upon them in all worlds and under all conditions. This Law of Unity is what in natural science is known as the Law of Continuity, and the Ancient Wisdom has embodied it in the Hermetic axiom "Sicut superius, sicut inferius; sicut inferius, sicut superius"—As above, so below; as below, so above. It leads us on from stage to stage, unfolding as it goes; and to this unfolding there is no end, for it is the Eternal Life finding ever fuller expression, as it can find more and more suitable channels through which to express itself. It can no more come to an end than numbers can come to an end.

But it *must* find suitable channels. Let there be no mistake about this. Perhaps some one may say: Cannot it *make* suitable channels for any sort of expression that it needs? The answer is, that it can, and it does so up to a certain point. As we have seen, the Word, Thought, or Initial Impulse of the Ever-Living Spirit starts a centre of cosmic activity in which the mathematical element of Law at once asserts itself; thenceforward everything goes on according to certain broad principles of sequence. This is a Generic Creation, creation according to *genera* or classes, like the "archetypal ideas" of Plato. This creation is governed by a Law of Averages, and the legal maxim "De minimis non curat lex"—the Law cannot trouble about minorities—applies to it. This generic law keeps the class going, and slowly advancing, simply as a class, but it can take no notice of individuals as such. As Tennyson puts it in "In Memoriam," speaking of Nature:

"So careful of the type she seems,
So careless of the single life."

This mode of creation reaches its highest level, at any rate in our world, in Genus Homo, or the human race. We also, as a race, are under the Law of Averages. The race continues to exist, but from the moment of birth the individual life is liable to be cut short in a hundred different ways. In producing man, however, Generic Creation has produced a *type* having a mental and physical constitution capable of perceiving the underlying principle of *all* creation, that is, of seeing the relation between the Word and the Law. We cannot conceive creation by type going further than this. By the nature of this type every human being has the potential of a further evolution, which will set it free from bondage to an impersonal Law of Averages, by specializing it through the Power of the Word, that is, by bringing the Personal Factor to bear upon the Impersonal Factor, and so unfolding the possibilities which can be achieved by their united activities. We have the power of using the Word so as to specialize the action of the Law, not by altering the Law, which is impossible, but by realizing its principle, and enabling it to work under conditions which are not spontaneously provided by Nature, but are provided by our own selection. The *capacity* for this exists in all human beings, but the practical application of this capacity depends on our recognition of the principles involved; and it is for this reason that I commenced this book by citing instances of the combined working of Law and Personality in purely physical science. I wanted first to convince the reader from well ascertained facts, that the Law contains infinite possibilities, but that this can only be brought out through the operation of the mind of man.

It is here that we find the value of the maxim "Nature unaided fails." The more we consider this maxim and the principle of Unity and Continuity, the clearer it will become, that Limitation is no part of the Law itself, but results only from our own limited comprehension of it; and that St. James uses no meaningless phrase, but is stating a logical and scientific truth, when he speaks of "The perfect Law of Liberty" (Jas. i, 25). What we have to do is, to follow this up, not by petulant self-assertion, but by quietly considering the why and wherefore of the whole thing. In doing so we can fortify ourselves with another maxim, that "Principle is not limited by Precedent." When we spread the wings of thought and speculate as to future possibilities, our conventionally-minded friends may say we are talking bosh; but if you ask them why they say so, they can only reply that the past experience of the whole human race is against you. They do not speak like this in the matter of flying-machines or carriages that go without horses; they say these are scientific discoveries. But when it comes to the possibilities of our own souls, they at once set a limit to the expansion of ideas, and do not see that the scientific principle of discovery is not confined to laboratory experiments. Therefore, we must not let ourselves be discouraged by such arguments. If our friends doubt our sanity, let them doubt it. The sanity of such men as Galileo and George Stephenson was doubted by their contemporaries, so we are in good company. At the same time we must not neglect to look after our own sanity. We must know some intelligible reason for our conclusions, and realize that however unexpected, they are the logical carrying out of principles which we can recognize in the Creation around us. If we do this we need not fear to spread the wings of fancy, even though some may not be able to accompany us; only we must remember that we are using wings. Fancy, in the ordinary acceptation of the word, has really no wings; it is like a balloon that just floats wherever any passing current of air may drive it. The possession of wings implies power to direct our flight, and fancy must be converted into trained Imagination, just as the helpless balloon has been superseded by navigable air-craft. It must be "the scientific imagination"; and the "scientific imagination" carried into the world of spiritual causation becomes the Word of Power, and its Power is derived from the fact that it is always working according to Law. Then we may go on confidently, because we are following the same universal principles by which all creation has been evolved, only now we are specializing its action from the standpoint of our own individuality, according to the ancient teaching that Man, the Microcosm, repeats in himself all the laws of the Macrocosm, or great world, around him.

As we begin to see the truth of these things, we begin to transcend the simply generic stage. That first stage is necessary to provide a starting-point for the next. The first stage is that of Bondage to Law. It could not be otherwise for the simple reason that you must learn the law before you can use it. Then from the stage of Generic Creation we emerge into that of individual Creation, in which we attain liberty through Knowledge of the Law of our own Being; so that it is not a mere theological myth to talk of a New Creation, but it is the logical outcome of what we now are, if, to our recognition of the Power of the Law we add the recognition of the Power of the Word.

CHAPTER V

THE SOUL OF THE SUBJECT

We may now turn to speculate a little on some conceivable application of the general principle we have been considering. It seems to me that, as a result of the generic creation of which I have just spoken, there is in everything what, for want of a better name, I may call "The soul of the subject."

Creation being by type, everything must have a *generic* basis of being in the Cosmic Law, not peculiar to that individual thing, but peculiar to the class to which it belongs, an adaptation of the Cosmic Soul for the production of all things belonging to that particular order, in fact, what makes them what they are and not something else. Now just because this basis is generic and common to the whole genus that is built upon it, it is not specific, but it acquires *localization through Form;* the form being that of the class to which it belongs, thus producing the individual of that class, whether a cat or a cabbage. It is this underlying *generic* being of the thing, that I want the student to understand by "the soul of the subject." In fact we may call it the Noumenon or essential being of the class, as distinguished from the specific characteristics that differentiate the individual from others of the same class. It follows from this that this *generic* soul has no individuality of its own, and consequently is open to receive impressions from any source that can penetrate the sheath of outward form and specific characteristic that envelopes it. At the same time it is a manifestation of Cosmic Law, and so cannot depart from its own class-nature, and therefore any influence that may be impressed upon it from some other source will always show itself *in terms of the sort of generic soul that is thus impressed;* for instance, it would be impossible so to impress a dog as to make it write a book; and we may therefore generalize the statement, and lay down the rule, that "Every *im*press receives *ex*pression in terms of the medium through which it is expressed." This becomes almost a self-obvious truism when put into plain language like this; thus, if I paint a picture in oils, my impression is conveyed in terms of this medium, and if I paint one in water-colours my conception will be conveyed in terms of that medium, and the methods of handling will be perfectly different in the two pictures.

This applies all round; and if we keep this generalization in mind, it will render many things clear, especially in psychic matters, which would otherwise seem puzzling.

Now we ourselves are included in the general creation, and consequently we have in us a generic or *type basis* of personality, which is entirely impersonal. This is not a contradiction in terms, though it may look like one. We belong to the class Genus Homo, the distinctive quality of which is Personality, that is to say, the possession of certain faculties which constitute us persons, and not things or animals; but at the same time this merely generic personality is common to all mankind, and is not that which distinguishes one individual from another, and in this sense it is impersonal; so we may call it our Cosmic or Impersonal Personality.

Now it is upon this cosmic element, inherent in all things from mineral to man, that Thought-Power acts, because, being impersonal, it has no private purpose of its own with which to oppose the suggestion that is being impressed upon it. The only thing is, that according to the rule just laid down, the response will always be in terms of the cosmic element which we have thus set in motion. Therefore on the human plane it will always be in terms of Personality.

The whole thing comes to this, that we impart to this impersonal element the reflection of our own personality, and thereby create in it a certain personality of its own, which will express itself in terms of the inherent nature of the impersonal factor, which we have thus temporarily invested with a personal quality; we are continually doing this unconsciously, either for good or ill; but when we come to understand the law of it, we must try so to regulate the habitual current of our thoughts, that even when we are not using this power intentionally, they may only exercise a beneficial influence.

In our normal state this cosmic element in ourselves is so closely united with our more conscious powers of volition and reasoning, that they constitute a single unity; and this is how it should be, only, as we shall see later on, with a difference. But there are certain abnormal states which are worth considering, because they make clearer the existence in us of this impersonal self, which in academical language is called the subliminal consciousness. The work of the subliminal consciousness exhibits itself in various ways, such as clairvoyance, clair-audience, and conditions of trance; all of which either occur spontaneously, or are induced by experimental means, such as hypnotism; but the similarity of the phenomena in either case shows, that it is the same faculty that is in evidence.

In those hypnotic experiments in which the operator merely makes the subject do some external act, we get no further than the fact that the person's individual will has been temporarily put to sleep, and that of the hypnotist has taken its place; still even this shows a power of impressing upon the subliminal consciousness a personal quality of its own, but it does not enable it to exhibit its own powers. The object of such experiments is, to exhibit the powers of the hypnotist, not to investigate the powers of the subliminal personality, which is of more importance in the present connection. But where the hypnotist employs his power of command to tell the subliminal self of the patient to exercise its own powers, merely directing it as to the subject upon which it is to be exercised, very wonderful powers indeed are exhibited. Places unknown to the percipient are accurately described; correct accounts are given of what people are doing elsewhere; the contents of sealed letters are read; the symptoms of disease are diagnosed and suitable remedies sometimes prescribed; and so on. Distance appears to make no difference. In many cases time also does not count, and historical events of long ago, with the details of which the seer had no acquaintance, are accurately described in all their minutiæ, which have afterwards been corroborated by contemporary documents. Nor are cases wanting in which events still future have been correctly predicted, as, for example, in Cazotte's celebrated prediction of the French Revolution, and of the fate that awaited each member of a large dinner-party when it should occur—though this was a spontaneous case, and not under hypnotism, which perhaps gives it the greater value.

The same powers are shown in spontaneous cases also, of which my own experiences related in a previous chapter may serve as a small example; but as there are many books exclusively devoted to the subject I need not go into further details here. If the reader be curious for further information, I would recommend him to read Gregory's "Letters on Animal Magnetism." It was published some fifty years ago, and, for all I know, may be out of print, but if the reader can procure it, he will find that it is a book to be relied upon, the work of a Professor of Chemistry in the University of Edinburgh, who investigated the matter calmly with a thoroughly trained scientific mind. But what I want the reader to lay hold of is the fact, that whether the action occur spontaneously or be induced by experimental means, these powers actually exist in us, and therefore in reckoning up the faculties at our disposal they must not be omitted.

In our more usual condition however, these faculties are subordinate to those which put us in touch with the every-day world, and I cannot help thinking, that at our present stage this is the best place for them. In this place they have a special function to perform, which I will speak of in another chapter, and in the meanwhile for my own part I should prefer to leave their development to the ordinary course of Nature, neither stimulating them by hypnotic influence, or auto-suggestion, nor repressing them if they manifest themselves of their own accord. However, every one must follow his or her own discretion in this matter; the only thing is, do not deny the existence of these faculties in yourself because you may not consciously exercise them, for they hold a very important place in our complex personality.

All such evidence on the subject as has come my way, appears to me to point to the fact, that it is through this impersonal or cosmic portion of our mind that Thought-Power operates upon us, whether in the form of telepathy, or of healing treatment, or in any other way; and it is through this channel also that thought currents, not specially directed towards ourselves, nevertheless affect us, just as the first wireless telephone message sent on September 29, 1915, from the office of the American Telephone Company in New York, and directed to San Francisco, was simultaneously heard at San Diego, at Darien in Panama, and even as far away as Pearl Island, Honolulu, in the Pacific Ocean.

We sometimes pick up messages which are not intended for us; so we must keep our receiver in perfect syntony of reciprocal vibration with the stations from which we require to receive messages, to the exclusion of others which would produce confusion.

But I have strayed a little from our present point, which is rather that of giving out influence than of receiving it. Through the instrumentality of this impersonal cosmic soul we can send out our Thought for the healing of disease, for the suggestion of good and happy ideas, and for many other beneficial purposes; though the extent of the result will of course be considerably influenced by the mental attitude of the recipient, which is therefore a factor to be reckoned with.

But this power of sending out a subtle influence, call it magnetism or what you will, is not confined to operations upon the human subject. Two ladies of my acquaintance experimented on two rose-trees, which, to all appearances, were both in equally good condition. They daily blessed one and cursed the other, with the result that at the end of a month the anathematized plant had withered up from the roots, while the other was in an abnormally flourishing condition. Nor are we entirely without scientific backing even in such a case as this; for Professor Bose tells us in his work on the "Response of Metals," that not only can they be poisoned by certain chemicals, so as to deprive them of their normal qualities, but that they can be mesmerized into a similar condition. Such facts as these therefore give considerable support to the theory of the existence in everything of a "soul of the subject," which responds after its own manner to the power of human thought.

In what manner, then, is this influence conveyed? It is here that our study of etheric waves comes to our assistance, by carrying the same principle further, and picturing the working of the known Law under unknown conditions. It will at least enable us to form a working hypothesis. I have stated that our actual commercial application of the etheric waves extends from the ultra-violet waves used in photography, and measuring only 1/254,000 of an inch, to those measuring many miles employed in wireless telegraphy; but this practical application by no means exhausts the conceivable possibilities of etheric vibrations; for not only do we find a gap of five octaves of as yet unknown waves between the dark heat group and the Hertzian group, but mathematically there is no limit to the greatness or smallness of the waves, and the scale may be prolonged indefinitely in either direction. Nor is this to be wondered at; for if we consider that vibration is not a progress of individual particles from one place to another, but the alternate rising and falling of the substance at the same point, and that the ether is a homogeneous and universally present substance, it is obvious that there is nothing to limit the minuteness or the greatness of the intervals at which the rising and falling will occur. Therefore we have an unlimited field for our imagination to play about in. Then, if we further reflect that all forms are built up of denser or finer aggregations of ether, and that what determines the generic form of anything is its cosmic soul, or the generating principle of the *class* to which it belongs, it follows that this soul must have a corresponding form, however inconceivably fine may be the etheric condensation which thus differentiates it from other souls, and prevents it from all being mixed up together in an indistinguishable mass. If now, we combine these two facts, that the soul of anything must have a form, however fine, and that there is no limit either to the greatness or the minuteness of etheric vibrations, we can draw certain deductions from these premises.

It is an established fact of ordinary science that, however closely particles of any substance may seem to cohere, they are in reality separated by interstices through which etheric waves can penetrate.

The principle may be illustrated by the power of the X-rays to penetrate apparently solid bodies, such as iron. Then, if we combine with this the fact, that there is no limit to the minuteness of etheric waves, we see that however fine may be the particles constituting any form, it is always possible to have etheric waves still finer and thus able to penetrate that form and set up vibrations in it. It is our familiarity with the denser modes of matter that makes it difficult for us to grasp the idea of these finer activities; but there is nothing in what we know of the denser modes to contradict the conception; on the contrary, it is just by what we have learned of these denser modes that we reach the principles on which these further conceptions are founded. Looking at this, therefore, in the light of a mathematical proposition, there is absolutely no limit to the fineness of any form, or to its susceptibilities to etheric vibrations.

Finally, to this add the power of the Word to start trains of etheric vibration, and you get the following series: The Word starts the etheric waves; these waves produce corresponding vibration in the soul of the subject; and the soul of the subject in turn communicates corresponding vibration to its body. We may thus explain the Creative Power of Thought on the basis of recognizable Law, and so we believe, because we know *why* we believe, not because somebody else has told us so. Doubt is still the creative action of Thought, only it is creating negatively; so it is helpful to feel that we have some reason for confidence in the Power of the Word. There are a great many "Thomases" among us, and as one of the number I shall be glad if I can help my "Brother Tommies" to get a grip of the why and wherefore of the things which appear at first sight so fantastic and improbable.

But the conception we are considering is not limited to concrete entities, whether persons or things. It applies to abstractions also, and it is for this reason that I have called it the "Soul of the Subject." We often speak of the "Soul of Music," or the "Soul of Poetry," and so on. Thus our ordinary talk stands on the threshold of a great mystery, which, however, is simple enough in practice. If you want to get a clearer view of any subject than you have at present, address yourself mentally to the abstract soul of that subject, and ask it to tell you about itself, and you will find that it will do so. I do not say that it will do this in any miraculous manner, but what you already know of the subject will range itself into a clearer order, and you will see connections that have not previously occurred to you. Then again, you will find that information of the class required will begin to flow towards you through quite ordinary channels, books, newspapers, or conversation, without your especially laying yourself out to hunt for it; and again, at other times, ideas will come into your mind, you do not know how, but illuminating the subject with a fresh light. I cannot explain how all this takes place. I can only say from personal experience that it happens. But of course we must not throw aside ordinary common-sense. We must sort out the information that comes to us, and compare it with our previous knowledge; in fact we must *work* at it: there is no premium for laziness. Nor must we expect to receive by a sudden afflatus a complete acquaintance with some subject of which we are entirely ignorant. I do not say that such a thing is altogether impossible, for I cannot venture to limit the possibilities of the Universe; but it is certainly not to be looked for in the ordinary course. I have sometimes been shown specimens of "inspirational painting" done by persons said to be entirely ignorant of art, and the ignorance is very apparent on the face of the work. I dare say an artist may be inspired in the production of a picture, but the technical training comes first, and the inspiration afterwards. The same I believe to be true of all other subjects, so that we come back to the maxim of the power always expressing itself in terms of the instrument through which it works. With this reservation, however, it appears to me, that every class of subject has a sort of soul of its own with which we can put ourselves *en rapport* by, so to say, mentally unifying our own personality with its abstract principle.

We are told by some teachers, that we can in the same way even construct entities in the nature of our Thought, and possessing a personality of their own with which we have endowed them. Whether this be the case I cannot say—I do not know all the secrets of the invisible. But if our thoughts do not create personal entities able to hang "on their own hook," they create forces which come to much the same thing. They start waves in the Universal etheric medium, which, like the electro-magnetic waves of telegraphy, spread all round from the point of initial impulse, and are picked up whenever a centre happens to be attuned to a similar rate of vibration, and each new centre energizes these vibrations again with a fresh impulse of its own; so in this way thought-currents become very real things.

Such, then, is the power of our Word, whether spoken or only dwelt upon in Thought, to impress itself upon the impersonal element around us, whether in persons or things. We cannot divest it of the power, though we may intensify its action by deliberate use of it, with knowledge of the principle involved, and therefore, whether consciously or unconsciously, we are sending out the influence of our personality all the time.

Now the more we know of these things the greater becomes our responsibility, and I would therefore solemnly warn the reader against any attempt to use the powers now indicated to the injury of any other person, or for the purpose of depriving any one else of that liberty of action which he would wish to enjoy himself. Such use of our mental powers is in direct opposition to the Law of Unity which I have spoken of; and since that Law is the basic principle of the whole Universe, any opposition to it places us in antagonism with a force immeasurably greater than ourselves.

Our Thought always continues to be creative; but in destructive use it becomes creative for destructive forces, and, since it has its origin in our own personality, we are certain sooner or later to feel its effects, on the principle that every action always produces a corresponding reaction. As we have seen, the Law knows nothing of persons, but acts automatically in strict accord with the nature of the power which has set it in motion. Under negative conditions the great Law of the Universe becomes your adversary, and must continue to be so, until by your altered mode of Thought you put yourself in line with it.

But on the other hand, if our intention be to co-operate with the Great Law, we shall find that in it also exists a mysterious "Soul of the Subject," which will respond to us, however imperfectly we may understand its *modus operandi*. It is the intention that counts, not the theoretical knowledge. The knowledge will grow by experience and meditation, and its value is measured entirely by the intention that is at the back of it.

CHAPTER VI

THE PROMISES

We have now, I hope, laid a sufficiently broad foundation of the relation between the Law and the Word. The Law cannot be changed, and the Word can. We have two factors, one variable, and the other invariable; so that from this combination any variety of resultants may be expected. The Law cannot be altered, but it can be specialized, just as iron can be made to float by the same law by which it sinks. Now let us try to figure out in our imagination an ideal of the sort of results we should want to bring out from these two factors.

In the first place I think we should like to be free from all worry and anxiety; for a life of continual worry is not worth living. And in the second we should like always to have something to look forward to and feel an interest in; for a life entirely devoid of all interest is also not worth living. But, granted that these two conditions be fulfilled, I think we should all be well pleased to go on living *ad infinitum*. Now can we conceive any combination of the Law and the Word which would produce such results? that is the question before us. The first step is to generalize our principle as widely as possible, for the wider the generalization, the larger becomes the scope for specialization. The invariable factor we already know. It is the Law, always creating in accordance with the Word that sets it in motion, whether constructive or destructive; so what we really have to consider is the sort of Word (i.e. Thought or Desire) which will set the Law working in the right direction. It must be a Word of confidence in its own power; otherwise by the hypothesis of the case it would be giving contradictory directions to the Law, or to borrow a simile from what we have learnt about waves in ether, it would be sending out vibrations that would cancel one another and so produce no effect. Then it must be a Word that does not compromise itself by antagonizing the Law of unity, and so producing disruptive forces instead of constructive ones. And finally, we must be quite sure that it really is the right Word, and that we have been making no mistake about it. If these conditions be fulfilled the logical result will be entire freedom from anxiety. Similarly with regard to maintaining a continued interest in life. We must have a continued succession of ideals, whether great or small, that will carry us on with something always just ahead of us; and we must work the ideals out, and not let them evaporate in dreams. If these conditions be fulfilled we have before us a life of never-ending interest and activity, and therefore a life worth living. Where then are we to find the Word which will produce these conditions: perfect freedom from anxiety and continual, happy interest? I do not think it is to be found in any way but by identifying our own Word with the Word which brings all creation into existence, and keeps it always moving onward in that continuous forward movement which we call Evolution. We must come back to the old teaching, that the Macrocosm is reproduced in the Microcosm, with the further perception that this identity of principle can only be produced by identity of cause. Law cannot be other than eternal and self-demonstrating, just as 2 × 2 must eternally = 4; but it remains only an abstract conception until the Creative Word affords it a field of operation, just as twice two is four remains only a mathematical abstraction until there is something for you to count; and accordingly, as we have already seen, all our reasoning concerning the origin of Creation, whether based on metaphysical or scientific grounds, brings us to the conception of a Universal and Eternal Living Spirit localizing itself in particular areas of cosmic activity by the power of the Word. Then, if a similar Creative Power is to be reproduced in ourselves, it must be by the same method: the localizing of the same Spirit in ourselves by the power of the same "Word." Then our Word, or Thought, will no longer be that of separate personality, but that of the Eternal Spirit finding a fresh centre from which to specialize the working of the Law, and so produce still further results than that of the First or simply Cosmic and Generic Creation, according to the two maxims that "Nature unaided fails," and that "Principle is not limited by Precedent."

I want to make this sequence clear to the student before proceeding further:

1. Localization of the Spirit in specific areas of Creative Activity.

2. Cosmic or Generic Creation, including ourselves as a race resulting from this, and providing both the material and the instruments for carrying the work further by *specializing the Original Creative Power* through individual Thought, just as in all cases of scientific discovery.

3. Then, since what is to be specialized through our individual Thought is the Word of the Originating Power itself, in order to do this we must think in terms of the Originating Word, on the general principle, that any power must always exhibit itself in terms of the instrument through which it works.

This, it appears to me, is a clear logical sequence, just as a tree cannot make itself into a box, unless there be first the idea of a box which does not exist in the tree itself, and also the tools with which to fashion the wood into a box; while on the other hand there could never be any box unless there be first a tree. Now it is just such a sequence as this that is set before us in the Bible, and I do not find it adequately set forth in any other teaching, either philosophical or religious, with which I am acquainted. Some of these systems contain a great deal of truth, and are therefore helpful as far as they go; but they do not go the whole way, and for the most part stop short at the first or simply Cosmic Creation; or, if they attempt to pass beyond this, it is on the line of making unaided power of the individual the sole means by which to do so, and thus in fact always keeping us at the merely generic level. Such a mode of Thought as this, fails to meet the requirements of our conception of a happy life as one entirely exempt from fear and anxiety. In like manner also it fails to meet the first requirements of the whole series, viz.: the Word should be certain of itself; and if it be not certain of itself we have no assurance that it may not eventually disappoint our hopes. In short, this mode of thought leaves us to bear the whole burden from which we want to escape. So it is not good enough; we must look for something better.

Now this something better I find in the *Promises* contained in the Bible, and it is this that to my mind distinguishes our own Scriptures from the sacred books of all other nations, and from all systems of philosophy. I do not at all ignore the current objections to the possibility of Divine Promises, but I think that on examination they will be found to be superficial and resulting from want of careful enquiry into the true nature of the Promises themselves. How is it possible for the Laws of the Universe to make exceptions? How can God act by individual favouritism unless it be either through sheer caprice, or by the individual managing to get round Him in some way, either by supplying some need which He cannot supply for Himself, in which case God is of limited power, or else by flattering Him, in which case He is the apotheosis of absurd vanity. The two are really the same question put in different ways—the question of individual exceptions to the general Law.

The answer is that there are no individual exceptions to the general Law; but there are very various degrees of realization of the Principle of the Law, and the more a man works with the Principle the more the Law will work for him; so that the finer his perception of the Principle becomes, the more he will appear to be an exception to the Law as commonly recognized.

Edison and Marconi are not capriciously favoured by the laws of Nature, but they know more about them than most of us.

Now it is just the same with the Bible Promises. They are Promises according to Law. They are based upon the widest generalization and hence lead to the highest specialization through the combined action of the Law and the Word—Jachin and Boaz, the Two Pillars of the Universe.

These Promises comprise all sorts of desirable things: health of body, peace of mind, earthly prosperity, prolongation of life, and, finally, even the conquest of death itself; but always on one condition: perfect "Confidence in the power of the All-Originating Spirit in response to our reliance on the Word." This is what the Bible calls Faith; and it is perfectly logical when we understand the principle of it, for every Thought of doubt is, in effect, the utterance of a Word which produces negative results by the very same law by which the Word of Faith produces positive ones. This is the only condition which the Bible imposes for the fulfilment of its Promises, and this is because it is inherent in the nature of the Law by which their fulfilment is to be brought about.

A few texts will suffice as examples of the Bible Promises, and no doubt most of my readers are familiar with many others; but it would be worth while to read the Bible through, marking all such texts, and classifying them according to the sort of promises they contain.

Read, for instance, Job xxii, 21, etc. This is a most remarkable passage containing among other things the promise of earthly wealth; or again Job v, 19, etc., where we find promises of protection in time of danger, power over material nature, and prolonged life. While in Job xxxiii, 23, etc., there is promise of return to youth, a promise which is repeated in Psalm ciii, 5. Again in Isaiah lxi, 20, etc., there is the promise of immensely extended physical life, death at the age of one hundred being counted so premature as to resemble that of an infant, and the normal standard of age being compared to a tree which lives for centuries; and the same passage also promises immediate answer to prayers. The Psalms are full of such promises, and they are scattered throughout the Bible.

Now there is an unfortunate tendency among people who read their Bible with reverence, to what they call "spiritualize" such passages as these, which means that they do not believe them. They say such things are impossible; and therefore they must have some other meaning, and accordingly they interpret the words metaphorically, as referring to something to be experienced in another life, but quite impossible in this one.

Of course there are spiritual equivalents to these things, and the teaching of the Bible is, that they are the outward correspondences of inward spiritual states; but to "spiritualize" them in the way I am speaking of, is nothing but unbelief in the power of God to work on the plane of Nature. How such readers square their opinion with the fact that God has created Nature, I do not know. Even in the animal world we find wonderful instances of longevity. If an elephant be not overworked before he is twenty, he is in full working power up to eighty, and will then be capable of light work for another twenty years, after which he may yet enjoy another twenty years of quiet old age as the reward of his labours, while crocodiles and tortoises have been known to live for centuries. If then such things be possible in the ordinary course of Nature in the animal world, why need we doubt the specializing power of the Word to produce far greater results in the case of man? It is because we will not accept the maxim, that "Principle is not limited by Precedent" in regard to ourselves, though we see it demonstrated by every new scientific discovery. We rely more on the past experience of the race, than on the Creative Power of God. We call Him Almighty, and then say that in His Book He promises things which He is not able to perform. But the fault is with ourselves. We limit "the Holy ONE of Israel," and as a consequence get only so much as by our mental attitude we are able to receive—again the old maxim that "Power can only work in terms of the instrument it works through." I do not say that it is at all easy for us to completely rid ourselves of negative race-thought ingrained into us from childhood, and subtly playing upon that generic impersonal self in us of which I have spoken, and which readily responds to those thought-currents to which we are habitually attuned. It is a matter of individual growth. But the promises themselves contain no inherent impossibility, and are logical deductions from the principles of the Creative Law.

If the power of the Spirit over things of the material plane be an impossibility, then by what power did Jesus perform his miracles? Either you must deny his miracles, or you must admit the power of the Spirit to work on the material plane—there is no way out of the dilemma. Perhaps you may say: "Oh, but He was God in person!" Well, all the promises affirm that it is God who does these things; so what it is possible for God to do at one time, it is equally possible for Him to do at all times. Or perhaps you hold other theological views, and will say that Jesus was an exception to the rest of the race; but, on the contrary, the whole Bible sets Him forth as the Example—an exception certainly to men as we now know them, but the Example of what we all have it in us to become—otherwise what use is He to us? But apart from all argument on the subject we have his own words, telling us that those who believe in Him, i.e., believe what He said about Himself—shall be able to do works as great as His own, and even greater (John xiv, 12). For these reasons it appears to me that on the authority of the Bible itself, and also on metaphysical and scientific grounds we are justified in taking such promises as those I have quoted in a perfectly literal sense.

Then there are promises of the power that will attend our utterance of the Word. "Thou shalt also decree a thing and it shall be established unto thee" (Job xxii, 28). "All things are possible unto you" (Mark ix, 23). "Whosoever ... shall believe that what he sayeth cometh to pass, he shall have whatsover he sayeth" (Mark xi, 23), and so on.

Other passages again promise peace of mind. "Thou wilt keep him in perfect peace whose mind is staid on Thee, because he trusteth in Thee" (Isaiah xxvi, 3). "Let him take hold of my strength that he may make peace with me" (Isaiah xxvii, 5). St. Paul speaks of "The God of Peace" in many passages, e.g., Rom. xv, 33; 2 Cor. xiii, 11; 1 Thess. v, 23, and Hebr. xiii, 20; and Jesus, in his final discourse recorded in the fourteenth, fifteenth and sixteenth chapters of St. John's Gospel, lays peculiar stress on the gift of Peace.

And lastly there are many passages which promise the overcoming of death itself; as for instance Job xix, 25-27; John viii, 51, and x, 28, and xi, 25 and 26; Hebr. ii, 14 and 15; 1 Cor. xv, 50-57; 2 Tim. i, 10; Rom. vi, 23 ("The gift of God is eternal life in Jesus Christ, our Lord").

"God commanded the blessing, even Life for evermore" (Ps. cxxxiii, 3).

Now I hope the reader will take the trouble to look up the texts to which I have referred, and not be lazy. I am sure he would do so if he were promised a ten pound note or a fifty dollar bill for his pains, and if these promises are not all bosh, there is something worth a good deal more to be got by studying them. Just run through the list: health, wealth, peace of mind, safety, creative power, and eternal life. You would be willing to pay a good premium to an Insurance Office that could guarantee you all these. Well, there is a Company that does this without paying any premium, and its name is "God and Co., Unlimited"; the only condition, is that you yourself have to take the part of "Co." and it is not a sleeping partnership, but a wide-awake one!

So I hope you will take the trouble to look up the texts; but at the same time you must remember that the reading of single texts is not sufficient. If you take any isolated phrase you choose, without reference to the rest of the Book, there is no nonsense you cannot make out of the Bible. You would not be allowed to do that sort of thing in a Court of Law. When a document is produced in evidence, the meaning of the words used in it are very carefully construed, not only in reference to the particular clause in which they occur, but also with reference to the intention of the document as a whole, and to the circumstances under which they were written. The same word may mean very different things in different connections; for instance I remember two reported cases in one of which the word "Spanish" meant a certain sort of leather, and in the other a kind of material used in brewing; and in like manner particular texts are to be interpreted in accordance with the gist of the Bible as a whole.

This is just the mistake the Jews made, of building up theories on particular texts, and which Jesus corrected when he said: "Search the Scriptures, for in them ye think ye have eternal life, and these are they which testify of me" (John v, 39), or, as the Revised Version puts it: "Ye search the Scriptures because ye think that in them ye have eternal life; and these are they which bear witness of me," which appears to be the better rendering. The words "ye think" is the key to the whole passage. He says in effect: "You fancy that eternal life is to be found in the book. It is not to be found in the book, but in what the book tells you about, and here I am as a living example of it." It is just the same with everything else. No book can do more than tell you about a thing; it cannot produce it. You may study the cookery book from morning till night, but that will not give you your dinner.

What Jesus meant was, that we should read the Scriptures in the same way we should read any other book of practical instruction. First think what it is all about; then look at the nature of the general principles involved, and then see what instruction the book gives you for their practical application. *Then go and do it.* And remember also a further difference between reading about a thing and doing it. A book is for everybody, and can therefore, only give general instruction; but when you come to do the thing you will always find it works with some personal modifications,—not departures from the general principles you have read about, but specializations of them—and in this way you will learn much that is not to be got out of books, even the best.

I remember many years ago, when I was much younger, asking one of our leading water-colour artists, [3] how he would recommend me to study landscape painting, and he said: "Practise continually from Nature, and you will learn more than any one can teach you; that is how I have learnt, myself." On the subject, then in question, he said just what Jesus did: "Here I am as a practical example of what I tell you." And another thing is, that the more you think principles out for yourself and try to observe them in practice, the clearer the meaning of your book will become to you. I have a few excellent books on painting, but I had no idea how excellent they were when I first got them; practical experience has taught me to find much more in them than I did at first, for now I understand better what they are talking about. Well, that is the way to read the Bible, neither despising it as worthless tradition, nor treating the mere letter of it with superstitious veneration; both extremes are to be equally avoided. In fact the Bible tells us so itself: "The letter killeth, but the Spirit giveth life" (2 Cor. iii, 6); this, of course, does not mean that the letter can be tampered with, any more than a judge can alter the wording of a document put in evidence; it must be interpreted in the general sense of the document as a whole; and when the letter is thus vivified by the Spirit, it will be found fully to express it. But we require to enter into the Spirit of it first.

Now it appears to me, that taken in this way, the Bible is an exceedingly practical book, and that is why I want the reader to get at some general principles which he will find, *mutatis mutandis*, equally applicable all round, whether to electricity, or to life, and whatever may be the subject-matter, it will always be found to resolve itself into a question of the relation between Law and Personality. If now we read the Bible Promises in the light of the general principles we have considered in the earlier pages, we shall find that they are all Promises according to Law. They are statements of the results to be obtained by a truer realization of the principles of Law and Personality than we have hitherto apprehended.

We must always bear in mind that the Law is set in motion by the Word. The Word does not *make* the Law, but gives it something to work upon, so that without the Word there could be no manifestation of the Law, a truth embodied in the maxim, that "Every Creation carries its own mathematics along with it." If the reader remembers what I have said in the chapter of "The Soul of the Subject," he will see that the principle involved, is that of the susceptibility of the Impersonal to suggestions from the Personal. This follows of course from the very Conception of Impersonality; it is that which has no power of selection and volition, and which is therefore without any power of taking an initiative on its own account.

In a previous chapter I have pointed out that the only possible conception of the inauguration of a world-system, resolves itself into the recognition of one original and universal Substantive Life, out of which proceeds a corresponding Verb, or active energy, reproducing in action what the Substantive is in essence. On the other hand there must be something for this active principle to work in; and since there can be nothing anterior to the Universal Life or Energy, both these factors must be potentially contained in it. If, then, we represent this Eternal Substantive Life by a circle with a dot in the centre, we may represent these two principles as emerging from it by placing two circles at equal distance below it, one on either side, and placing the sign "+" (plus) in one, and the sign "-" (minus) in the other. This is how students of these subjects usually map out the relation of the *prima principia*, or first abstract principles. The sign "+" (plus) indicates the Active principle, and the sign "-" (minus) the Passive principle. If the reader will draw a little diagram as described, it will help to make what follows clearer.

Necessarily the initiative must be taken by the Active principle; and the taking of initiative implies selection and volition, that is to say, the essential qualities of personality; and Passivity implies the converse of all this, and therefore is Impersonality. The two principles in no way conflict with one another, but are polar opposites, like the positive and negative plates of a battery, or the two ends of a magnet. They are complementary to one another, and neither can work without the other. A little consideration will show that this is not a mere fancy, but a self-obvious generalization, the contrary to which it is impossible to conceive. It is simply the case of the box which cannot come into existence without the activity of the carpenter and the passivity of the wood.

From such considerations as this the deep thinkers of old times posited the generating of a world-system by the interaction of what they named Animus Dei, the Active principle, and Anima Mundi, or Soul of the Universe, the Passive principle—the one Personal, and the other Impersonal; and by the hypothesis of the case the only mode of activity possible to Anima Mundi is response to Animus Dei. But the same impersonal passivity must also make Anima Mundi receptive likewise to lesser and more individualized modes of Personality, and it becomes, so to say, fecundated by the ideas thus impressed upon it. In every case "the word is the seed." We may picture this planting of an idea or "word" in the Cosmic soul as acting very much like the initial impulse that starts a train of waves in ether, and these thought-waves are reproduced in corresponding forms; or, to recur to the simile of seed, the cosmic soul acts like the soil and gives it nourishment. Looking at it in this way the old exponents of these things regarded the Active principle as Masculine, and the Passive as Feminine, the one generating and the other nutritive, corresponding to the words *rouah* and *hoshech*, the expansion and compression principles in the Hebrew text of the opening verses of Genesis.

If then we posit this impersonal Soul of the Universe as the living principle dwelling in the substance of the etheric Universal Medium it will account for a good many things. If it be asked why we should assume the presence of a living principle in the Universal Substance the answer is in the maxim "Quod ex Vivo Vivum," what proceeds from Life is living. Then as we see by our diagram, Anima Mundi equally with Animus Dei proceeds from the original Substantive of Life, and therefore, on the principle of the above maxim, that like produces like, Anima Mundi must also be a living thing whose vehicle is the Universal Substance.

We may picture then, the response of the indwelling Soul of the Universal Medium to our Thought, as starting corresponding vibrations in the Substance of the Medium, just as our own thought, acting through the vibratory system of our nerves, causes our body to make the movement we intend. But perhaps you will say: How can this be, seeing that by the hypothesis the Soul of the Universe is Impersonal, and therefore unintelligent? Well, it is just this fact of having no thought of its own, that enables us to impress our thought upon it and cause it, so to say, to "take on" an intelligence relatively to the subject of our thought, much in the same way that the impersonal soul in the human subject "takes on" or reflects the thought of the hypnotist, and not infrequently develops it to a far greater extent than the original thought of the operator expressed. Such a hypothesis—and I think some such hypothesis is needed to account for any creation at all—throws light on the *modus operandi* of the Bible Promises. We plant the Word of the Promise in the womb of Anima Mundi, and if we do not uproot it by using the same power adversely, it is bound to come to fruition in due course, by the same Law by which the world-systems are formed; and if we are to believe that the Word of the Promise is not our own word, but the Word of God, then our Thought of it is imbued with a corresponding power as we hand it over to Anima Mundi. Thus the Promises fulfil themselves automatically, in accordance with the principles of the relations between Law and Personality, and they do so, *not in our own power*, but by the Power of the Word of God.

This, then, gives us at least an intelligible working hypothesis of the rationale of the Bible Promises. The measurement of their fulfilment is exactly proportional to our belief in them, not from any unintelligible cause, and still less from any unreasoning feat of a capricious Deity, but by the working of an intelligible Law. If any of my readers happens to be an electrician, he will find an exact parallel in what is known as Ohm's Law. Such readers will be familiar with the formula $C = E/R$, but for the benefit of those to whom this formula may be unintelligible, I will give a few words of explanation. C means the current of electricity which is to be delivered for any work that is to be done. E stands for the Electro-motive force which generates the current; and R is the Resistance offered to the current by the conductor, such as the wires through which it flows. If there be no resistance, the full amount of current generated would be delivered. But without any conductor no current could be delivered, and therefore there must be *some* resistance, and so the full power of the Electro-motive force can never be delivered by the Current. The amount that will be delivered is the original power of the Electro-motive force divided by the Resistance. The Resistance therefore acts as a restricting force, limiting the extent to which the power of the original Electro-motive force shall be delivered at the point where the work is to be done, but at the same time no delivery at that point could be effected without it; so the Resistance also has a necessary part to play in the working of the circuit. Now if we want to translate the formula $C = E/R$ into terms of spiritual force we may put it thus: E stands for the limitless Potential of the Eternal Spirit; C stands for the current flowing from it; and R stands for the localizing quality of our thought. We cannot entirely dispense with this localizing quality, for our whole purpose is to transmute the *unlimited,* undifferentiated power, which subsists in the Eternal Substantive of Spirit, into a particular differentiated mode of action, which therefore implies a corresponding centralization. This is the proper function of our thought. It is this compressing power which, as I said above, the Hebrew renders by the word "*hoshech*" in the opening verses of Genesis, and which is the necessary complementary to the converse expanding power or "*rouah.*" It takes the co-operation of the two to produce any results.

Restricted, then, to its proper function our R or condensing quality is an essential factor in the work. But if it be allowed to take the form of doubt or unbelief, then it renders the flow of the current from the Spirit ineffective to the extent to which the doubt is entertained; and if doubt be allowed to degenerate into total unbelief and denial of the Power of the Spirit, we thereby cancel the originating force altogether. To put it in terms of the electrical formula, we make R greater than E, in which case no current can flow. We thus find that the words "According to your faith be it unto you" are actually the statement of a Mathematical Law, having nothing vague about them. This may be a somewhat original application of Ohm's Law, but the parallel is so exact, that I cannot help thinking it will appeal to some of my readers who may be conversant with Electrical Science. For those who are not, a simpler simile may be, that you cannot deliver a more powerful stream of water than the bore of the pipe through which it flows will admit of; or, to employ a legal truism, delivery on the part of the donor must be met by acceptance on the part of the donee before a deed of gift can become operative; or, in still simpler language, "you may take a horse to the water but you can't make him drink."

We see, then, that there is a Law of Faith, and that Faith is not a denial of the universal reign of Law, but the perception of its widest generalization, and therefore giving scope to its highest specialization. The opposition between Faith and Law, of which St. Paul so often speaks, is the opposition between this broad view of the ultimate Principle of the Creative Law and that narrower view of restriction by particular laws, which prevents us from grasping the Law of Faith; but that he does not deny the *Principle* of Law, that is the relation between C and E, is clear from his own statement in Rom. viii, where he says: "The Law of the Spirit of Life in Christ Jesus sets me free from the law of Sin and Death;" in other words: the Law of the Good sets us free from the Law of Evil; and for the same reason St. James says, that the perfect law is the law, of Liberty (Jas. i, 25).

Of course if we suppose that faith is something contrary to the law of the Universe we at once import into our thought the negative quality which entirely vitiates our action. We rightly perceive that the laws of the Universe can never be altered, and if our notion of Faith be, that it is an attempt to work in contradiction to these laws, the best definition we can give it is that given by the little girl in the Sunday school, who said that "Faith is trying to make yourself believe what you know is not true." The reason for such a misconception is, that it entirely omits one of the factors in the calculation. It considers, only the Law, and gives no place to the Word in the scheme of things. Yet we do not carry this misconception into the sciences of chemistry and electricity. We take the immutability of the Law as the basis of these sciences, but we do not expect the immutable Law to produce a photographic apparatus, or an electric train, without the intervention of a reasoning and selective power which specializes the fundamental general Law into particular uses. We do not look to the Law for those powers of reasoning and selection, through which we make it work in all the highly complex ways of our ordinary commercial applications of it—we know better than that. We look to Personality for this. In our every-day pursuits we always act on the maxim that "Nature unaided fails," and that the infinite possibilities stored up in the Law, can only be brought to light by a power of reasoning and selection working through the Law. This co-operation of the Personal with the Impersonal is the Law *of* the Law; and since the Law is unchangeable, this Law *of* the Law must also be unchangeable, and must therefore apply on all planes, and through all time—the Law, that without co-operation of the Law and the Word nothing can be brought into existence, from a solar system to a pin; while on the other hand there is no limit to what can be got out of the Law by the operation of the Word.

If the student will look at the Bible Promises in the light of the general principles, he will find that they are perfectly logical, whether from the metaphysical or from the scientific standpoint, and that their working is only from the same Law through which all scientific developments are made. If this be apprehended it will be clear that the Word of Faith is not "trying to make ourselves believe what we know is not true," but, as St. Paul puts it, it is "giving substance to things not yet seen" (Heb. xi, 1, R.V.).

CHAPTER VII

DEATH AND IMMORTALITY

I think most of my readers will agree with me, that the greatest of all the promises is that of the overcoming of death, for, as the greater includes the less, the power which can do *that* can do anything else. We think that there are only two things that are certain in this world—death and taxes, and no doubt, under the ordinary past conditions, this is quite true; but the question is: are they really inherent in the essential nature of things; or are they not the outcome of our past limited, and often inverted modes of Thought? The teaching of the Bible is that they are the latter. On the subject of taxes the Master says: "Render unto Cæsar the things that are Cæsar's" (Matth. xxii, 21), but on another occasion he said that the children of the King were not liable to taxation (Matth. xvii, 26). However we may leave the "taxes" alone for the present, with the remark that their resemblance to death consists in both being, under present conditions, regarded as compulsory. Under other conditions, however, we can well imagine "taxes" disappearing in a unity of thought which would merge them in co-operation and voluntary contribution; and it appears to me quite possible for death to disappear in like manner.

In whatever way we may interpret the story of Eden, whether literally, or if, like some of the Fathers of the church such as Origen, we take it as an allegory, the result is the same—that Death is not in the essence of man's creation, but supervened as the consequence of an inverted mode of thinking. The Creative Spirit thought one way, and Eve thought another; and since the Thought of the Creating Spirit is the origin of Life, this difference of opinion naturally resulted in death. Then, from this starting-point, all the rest of the Bible is devoted to getting rid of this difference of opinion between us and the Spirit of Life, and showing us that the Spirit's opinion is truer than ours, and so leading us to adopt it as our own. The whole thing turns on the obvious proposition, that if you invert the cause you also invert the effect. It is the principle that division is the inversion of multiplication, so that if $2 \times 2 = 4$ then you cannot escape from the consequence that $4/2 = 2$. The question then is, which of the two opinions is the more reasonable—that death is essentially inherent in the nature of things, or that it is not?

Probably ninety-nine out of a hundred readers will say, the whole experience of mankind from the earliest ages proves that Death is the unchangeable Law of the Universe, and there have been no exceptions. I am not quite sure that I should altogether agree with them on this last point; but putting that aside, let us consider whether it really is the essential Law of the Universe. To say that this is proved by the past experience of the race, is what logicians call a *petitio principii*—it is assuming the whole point at issue. It is the same argument which our grandfathers would have used against aerial navigation—no one had ever travelled in the air, and that proved that no one ever could. My father, who was a junior officer in India when the first railway was run in England, used to tell a story of one of his senior officers, who, on being asked what he thought of the rapidity of the new mode of travelling, said he thought it was "all a damned lie," which opinion appeared to him to settle the whole question. But I hope that none of my readers will hold the same opinion regarding the overcoming of death, even though they might express it in more polite language. At any rate it may be worth while to examine the theoretical possibility of the idea.

To begin with, it involves a self-contradiction to say that the energy of any force can stop the working of that force. If a force stops working, it is for one of two reasons, either that the supply of it is exhausted, or that it is overcome by an opposite and neutralizing force. But we have seen that the Originating Cause of all things can only be an inexhaustible Power of Life, and therefore the hypothesis of it becoming exhausted is eliminated; and similarly, since all the forces of the Universe proceed from this Source, it is impossible for any of them to have a nature diametrically opposite to that of the source from which they flow. So the alternative must be eliminated also. Accordingly, the outflow, undifferentiated, of Life and Energy from the Eternal Substantive of Spirit, is never stopped *by its own current* in any of its differentiated streams; it is impossible for a current to be stopped by its own flow, whether it be a current of electricity, steam, water, or anything else. What then does stop the flow of any sort of current? It is the Resistance or *inertia* of the channel through which it flows; so that we come back to the formula of Ohm's Law, $C = E/R$ as a general proposition applicable to any conceivable sort of energy.

The neutralizing power then, is not that of the flowing of any sort of energy, but the rigidity, or inertia of the medium through which the energy has to make its way; thus bringing us back to *rouah* and *hoshech,* the expansive and compressive principles of the opening verses of Genesis. It is the broad scientific generalization of the opposition between Ertia, or Energy, and Inertia, or Absence of Energy; and since, for the reasons just given, Ertia cannot go against itself, the only thing that can stop it is Inertia.

Now the components of the human body are simply various chemical elements—so much carbon, so much hydrogen, etc., as any textbook on the subject will tell you; and although, of course, every sort of substance is the abode of ceaseless *atomic* energy, we all recognize that merely atomic energy is not that of the powers of thought, will, and perception, which make us organized mentalities instead of a mere aggregation of the various substances exposed to view in a biological museum, as constituting the human body—you might take all these substances in their proper proportions, and shake them up together, but you would not make an intelligent man of them. We are therefore safe in saying that the physiological body represents the principle of inertia in us, while the something that thinks in us represents the principle of Ertia.

The balance of power between the Life Principle in us and the Death Principle, is then, necessarily, a question of the balance between these two, the spirit and the flesh, or ertia and inertia.

Why then does the balance preponderate to the life-side for a certain length of time, and then go over to the opposite side?

Now this brings us to the distinction which the old writers drew, between the "Vital Soul" of any living thing and the Spirit. Their conception of the "Vital Soul" was very much the same as I have set forth in the chapter on "The Soul of the Subject." It is the individual's particular share of the Cosmic Soul or Anima Mundi, whether it be an individual tree, or an individual person; and the ordinary maximum length of time, during which the Vital Soul will be able to overcome the inertia of its physical vehicle, depends upon the particular class to which the individual belongs. What the ordinary maximum is in regard to any species is a matter of experience, and it is in this way that we have fixed the usual limit of human life at three-score years and ten.

Now it is here that we shall begin to profit by some knowledge about the invisible part of ourselves. The actual molecules of our body, as I have just said, are only so much dead matter. This inert material is pulled about in various directions by strings which we call muscles, according to the movements we wish our bodies to make, and these muscles are set in motion by the vibrations of the nerves. [4] But what is it that occasions these vibrations of the nerves? Here we begin to pass beyond the limits of official Science, though not beyond the limits of recognizable Law. We have to recognize the existence of an etheric body acting as an intermediary between intention, desire, or (in the case of human beings) thought of the soul and the physical vibrations of the nerves. This is why, in an earlier chapter, I have drawn attention to our power of sending out etheric vibrations beyond the limits of the physical body, as in the case of De Rocha's experiments. Such experiments show that there is in us something not composed of dense matter, which is able to convey vibrations to dense matter; and it is this something which we speak of as the etheric body.

But if we wish to trace the links by which our thought operates upon the physical body, we find ourselves compelled to postulate yet another intermediary, what I have spoken of as the "Vital Soul"—a vehicle which does not *consciously think*, but in which what we may call race-consciousness becomes centred in the individual. This race-consciousness is none other than the ever-present "will-to-live" which is the basis of physical evolution—that automatically acting principle—which causes plants to turn towards the sun, animals to seek their proper food, and both animals and men to try instantly to escape from immediate danger. It is what we call instinct which does not reason. I may give a laughable experience of my own to illustrate the fact that conscious reason is not the method of this faculty. Once when on leave from India I was walking along a street in London in the heat of a summer's day and suddenly noticed just at my feet a long dark thing apparently wriggling across the white glare of the pavement. "Snake!" I exclaimed, and jumped aside for all I was worth, and the next moment was laughing at myself for not recollecting that cobras were not common objects in the London streets. But it looked just like one, and of course turned out to be nothing but a piece of rag. Well, instinct did its duty even if it did make a fool of me; but there is certainly no conscious reasoning in the matter, only the automatic action of inherent Law—"Self-preservation is the first law of Nature."

This Vital Soul, then, is the seat of all those instincts which go towards the preservation of the individual's physical body, and towards the propagation of the race; and it is on this account that our theosophical friends call it the "Desire Body" or, to use the Indian term "Kama rupa." It acts with conscious intention, but not with conscious *reasoning*. It is thus distinguished on the one hand from the etheric body, which is a mere vehicle for finer vibrations than can take place in the denser matter of the physical body, but which has *no intention*; and on the other from the *mind* which acts by conscious reasoning, and it thus forms an intermediary between the two.

The importance of recognizing the place of this higher intermediary in the ascending scale of living principle is, that for all practical purposes the animal world does not rise higher than this in the scale. It is true that in particular instances we find the first dawning of the mental faculty in an animal, but it is only very faint; so this does not affect the broad general principle. The point to be noted is that up to this stage human beings are built on the same lines as animals, and what distinguishes us, is the addition in ourselves of a higher factor,—that of the reasoning mind exercising the power of conscious thought.

Now it is the direction of this thought that influences the three lower factors. The sequence, going upwards, is as follows:—movement is communicated to the physical body by the etheric body; and movement is communicated to the etheric body by the Vital Soul; then, in proportion as the purely instinctive action of the Vital Soul is controlled by the conscious thought, so its action upon the two lowest principles is modified.

Here, then, is the crucial point. In what direction is the conscious thought going to modify the action of the three principles that are below it? If it takes the soul of mere racial desire and the physical body as its standard of thought, then it naturally follows that it cannot raise it any higher. It has descended to *their* level and so cannot pour any stream of life into it, on the simple principle that no current can ever flow from a lower to a higher level, whether the difference in level be that of actual elevation, as in the case of water, or different in potential, as in the case of electricity. On the other hand if the conscious mind recognizes that itself proceeds from some higher source, it looks to receive life from that source, and its thought is modified accordingly, and in turn re-acts correspondingly upon the lower principles.

If this is clear to the student, he will now see how it is that by limiting our conception of life to the current ideas entertained by the race, we impress these ideas on our three lower principles. It is true that these three principles are not capable of reasoning themselves, but the highest of them, the Vital Soul, has its action modified by the reasoning principle above it, and so communicates to the two lowest principles corresponding waves of vibration. And in this connection we must remember the distinction between the two systems of nerves; the voluntary system connected with the brain and forming the medium of all voluntary action, and the involuntary, or sympathetic system connected with the solar plexus and controlling all the automatic actions of the body, and thus being the agent of that continual renewal of the physical organism which is always going on, and keeps in existence for a life time a body which begins to disintegrate immediately the soul has left it. [5] Now it is through this inner Builder of the Body that our Thought re-acts upon our physical organism. The response is purely automatic, for the simple reason that there is no original thinking power in the three lower principles; the action is that of the Law as directed by Thought or Word.

In this way then, it appears to me, the Personal in us acts upon the Impersonal in us; and if we assume, as I think we may, that this action takes place by means of etheric waves, we have, on general scientific principles, a clue to what we read in the Bible about the transmutation of the body. The theory of the constitution of the atom shows us that its nature is determined by the number of its particles and their rate of revolution, and that a change in the rate of revolution results in the throwing off of some of the particles. Then the number of particles being altered, there results a change in the distribution of the positive and negative charges within the sphere of the atom, since they must always exactly balance one another; and this change in the distribution of the positive and negative charges must instantly result in a corresponding change in the geometrical configuration of particles constituting the atom.

That the particles automatically arrange themselves into groups of different geometrical form within the sphere of the atom, has been demonstrated both mathematically and experimentally by Professor J.J. Thompson, [6] these geometrical forms resulting of course from the balance of attraction and repulsion between the positive and negative charges of the particles.

That the transmutation of one substance into another is not a mere dream of the mediæval alchemists is now already shown by Modern Science. Under suitable conditions an atom of Radium breaks down into atoms of another sort known as Radium Emanations, and these again break down into yet another sort of atoms to which the name of Radium Emanations X has been given, while Radium Emanation also gives rise to the atom of Helium (N.K. 124). Thorium also behaves in the same manner, transmuting into atoms called Thorium X, which again change into atoms of another sort to which the name of Thorium Emanations has been given and these in turn transmute into atoms of yet another kind, known as Thorium Emanations X. The same is the case also with Uranium which, however, so far as is yet known, undergoes only one transmutation into what is known as Uranium X.

The transmutation of one sort of atom into another is therefore not a mere visionary fancy, but an established fact; and although our laboratory experiments in this direction may not as yet have gone very far, they have gone far enough to show that a Law of Transmutation does exist in Nature. Then, since the difference between one sort of atom and another results from the difference and arrangement of their particles, and the difference in the number and arrangement of the particles results from the difference in the speed of their rotation, and this again results from the difference in the energy or rate of vibration of the particles, we come back to different rates of etheric vibrations as the commencement of the whole series of changes; and as is proved by the facts of wireless telephoning, different rates of etheric vibrations can be set in motion by the varying sounds of the human voice, even on the physical plane. May it not be then, that by the same law, vibrations of other wavelengths, yet unknown to science, will be set in motion by the unspoken word of our thought?

The substance known as Polonium, even by its near approach to an electric bell, causes it to ring, and if etheric waves can thus be started by an inanimate substance, why should we suppose that our thought has less power, especially when metaphysically we cannot avoid the conclusion that the whole creation must have its origin in the Divine Thought?

From such considerations as these, I think we may reasonably infer that if the mind be illuminated by a range of thought coming from a higher mind, there is no limit to the power which may thus be exercised over the material world, and that therefore St. Paul's statement regarding the transmutation of the present physical body, is one which should be included in the circle of our ideas, as being within the scope of the Laws of the Universe when their action is specialized by the power of the Word (1 Cor. xv); and similarly with regard to other statements to the same effect contained in the Bible. What is wanted is the realization of a greater Word than that which we form from the current experience of the race. The race has formed its Word on the basis of the lower principles of our being, and if we are to advance beyond this, the Law of the subject clearly indicates that it can only be by adopting a more fundamental Word, or Idea, than that which we have hitherto thought to include the entire range of possibilities. The Law of our further Evolution demands a Word not formed from past experiences, but based upon the eternal principle of the All-Originating Life itself. And this is in strict accord with scientific method. If we had always allowed ourselves to be ruled by past experiences we should still be primitive savages; and it is only by the gradual perception of underlying principles, that we have attained the degree of civilization we have reached to-day; so what the Bible puts before us is simply the application to the life in ourselves of the maxim that "Principle is not limited by Precedent."

Now the Bible Promises serve to put us on the track of this Principle: they suggest lines of enquiry. And the enquiry leads to the conclusion that the two ultimate factors are the Law and the Word. What we have missed hitherto is the conception of the limitless possibilities of the Law, and the limitless power of the Word. On one occasion the Master said to the Jews "Ye know not the Scriptures neither the power of God" (Matth. xxii, 29) and the same is the case with ourselves. The true "Scripture" is the "scriptura rerum" or the Law indelibly written in the nature of things, and the written Scriptures are true only because they contain the statement of the Principle of the Law. Therefore until we see the Principle of the Law we "know not the Scriptures." On the other hand, until we see the Principle of the operation of the Word through the Law, we do not know "the Power of God"; and it is only as we come to perceive the interaction of the Law and the Word that we see the beginning of the way that leads to Life and Liberty.

But although it is evident from the text just quoted, as well as from other intimations in his Epistles, that St. Paul fully grasped the principle of the transmutation of the body, he himself tells us that he has not yet realized it in practice. He says he has not yet "attained to the resurrection from the dead," but is still pressing on towards its attainment (Ph. iii, 12). And it is to be remarked that he is not here speaking of a general "resurrection *of* the dead," but, as the word *exanastasis* in the original Greek indicates, of a special resurrection from among the dead; this indicates an *individual* achievement, not merely something common to the whole race. From this and other passages it is evident that by "the dead" it means those whose conception of Life is limited to the four lower principles, thus **unifying** the mind with the three principles which are below it; and the same idea is expressed in a variety of ways all through the Bible. This therefore shows that he is quite aware that knowledge of a principle does not enable us then and there to attain the completeness of the application, and if this be the case with St. Paul, we cannot be surprised to find it the same with ourselves. But on the other hand knowledge of the principle is the first step towards getting it to work.

Well, St. Paul is dead and buried, and so I suppose will most of us be in a few years; so the question confronts us, what becomes of us then?

As Milton puts it in "Il Penseroso" we want:

"to unsphere
The spirit of Plato and unfold
What worlds or what vast regions hold
The immortal mind that hath forsook
Her mansion in the fleshly nook."

Yes, this is a question of deep personal interest to us; but as I cannot speak from experience, I will restrict myself to seeing whether we can form any sort of general hypothesis on the basis of the principles we have recognized. What then is likely to survive? The physical body is of course disintegrated by the chemistry of Nature. The etheric body probably continues to retain its form longer, because it is a condensation of etheric particles wrought together by the etheric waves sent out by the Vital Soul, and is therefore not subject to the laws of chemical affinity. The Vital Soul, being the race-principle of life in the individual,—that principle which automatically seeks to preserve the individual from disintegration,—probably survives longer still, until, ceasing to receive any reflex vibrations from the body, it grows gradually weaker in its sense of individual guardianship, and so is eventually absorbed into the group-soul or generic essence of the class to which it belongs. This is probably what happens in the case of animals for want of any higher vivifying principle, and would be the same with us were it not for the fact of having such a higher principle. In our case I should imagine that the influx of etheric waves, received from the thought action of the mind, would have the effect of continuing to impress the Vital Soul with a sense of individuality, in terms of its own plane, which would prevent it from being absorbed into the group-soul so long as the vital current from the mind continued to reach it. But eventually that current would cease to reach it, and in some cases, because the individual mind that governed it would gradually realize that its connection with the physical plane had ceased, and in others, because through a higher illumination the mind had, of its own volition, turned its thought in another direction. In either case, on the ceasing of the influx of that vitalizing current, the Vital Soul of the human being would likewise be absorbed into the Cosmic Soul, or Anima Mundi.

How long the processes of the disintegration of the etheric body, and absorption of the vital soul may take, is a question on which I can offer no opinion beyond saying that certain psychic phenomena suggest that in some cases they may take a long period of time. But for the reasons I have now given, it appears to me that the permanently surviving factor is the thinking mind which is our real self, and is positively our centre of consciousness after the physical body has been put off.

By the facts of the case its consciousness is no longer affected by vibrations received from the physical body; and therefore, to the extent to which our idea of life has been centred in that body, we shall feel its loss. If our motto has been "Let us eat and drink, for tomorrow we die" we shall feel very dead indeed—a living death, a consciousness of being cut off from all that constituted our enjoyment of life—a thirst for the satisfaction of our customary ideas, which we have no power to quench; and, in proportion as our habitual mode of thought is raised above that lowest level, so will our sense of loss be less. Then, by the same Law, if our habitual mode of thought is turned towards pure, beautiful, and helpful ideals, we shall feel no loss at all, for we shall carry our own ideals with us, and, I hope, see them more clearly by reason of their disentanglement from mundane considerations. In what precise way we may then be able to work out our ideals I will not now stop to discuss. What we want first is a reasonable theory, based upon the principle of that universal Law which is only varied in its actions by the conditions under which it works; so, instead of speculating as to precise details, we may generalize the question of how we can work out the good ideals which we carry over with us, and put it this way:—Our ideas are embodied in thoughts; thoughts start trains of etheric waves, which waves induce reciprocal action whenever they meet with a receiver capable of vibrating synchronously with them, and so eventually the thought becomes a fact, and our helpful and beautiful ideal becomes a work of power, whether in this world or in any other.

Now it is to the forming of such ideals that the Bible, from first to last is trying to lead us. From first to last it is working upon one uniform principle, that the Thought is the Word, that the Word sets in motion the Law, and that when the Law is set in motion it acts with mathematical precision. The Bible is a handbook of instruction for the use of our Creative Power of Thought, and this is the sequence which it follows—one definite method, so fundamental in its nature, that it applies equally to the making of a packing-case or the making of a solar system.

Now we have formed a generalized conception, based on this universal method, of the sort of consciousness we are likely to have when we pass out of the physical body. Then our thought naturally passes on to the question what will happen after this?

It is here that some theory of the reconstitution of the physical body appears to me to hold a most important place in the order of our evolution. Let us try to trace it out on the general lines of the Creative Power of Thought indicated above, the keynote to which is that the Law is specialized by the Word, and cannot of itself bring out the infinite possibilities contained in it without such specializing, just as in all scientific development of ordinary life. The clue to the whole question is, that our place in the Universal Order is to develop the infinite resources of the Original Life and Substance into actual facts. "Nature unaided fails." The Personal Factor must co-operate with the Impersonal, alike for setting up an electric bell, or for the furtherance of cosmic evolution; and the reason it is so is, because it could not possibly be otherwise.

If now we start by recognizing this as our necessary place in the Progressive Order of the Universe, I think it will help us to form a reasonable theory as to the reconstruction of the body. First of all, why have we any physical body at all? As a matter of fact we have one, and no amount of transcendental philosophizing will alter the fact, and so we may conclude that there is some reason for it. We have seen the truth of the maxim "Omne vivum ex vivo," and therefore that all particular forms of life are differentiations of the one Basic Life. This means a localizing of the Life-Principle in individual centres. The formation of a centre implies condensation; for where there is no condensation the Energy, whether electricity or Life, is simply *dispersed* and *achieving no purpose*. Therefore distinctness from the undifferentiated Original Life is a necessity of the case. Consequently the higher the degree of Consciousness of Individuality, the greater must be the Consciousness of *Distinctness of Personality*.

We say of a "wobbly" sort of person: "That fellow is no use, you can't depend on him." We say of a person whose ideas, intentions, and methods are subject to continual variations under all sorts of outside influences, whether of opinions or circumstances, that he has "no backbone," meaning that he is in want of individuality. He has no real thought of his own, and so has no Word of Power by which to co-operate with the Law; therefore, to the extent to which this is the case with any of us, we are of no use in furthering the unfoldment of Evolution, whether in ourselves or anywhere else.

Now we talk a lot about Evolution or the *un*-folding, but we seem often not to realize that there must be something to unfold; and that therefore *In*-volution, or the concentration of the Life-principle, must be a condition precedent to its *E*-volution. This process of Involution must therefore be a process of gradually increasing concentration of the Life-principle, by association with denser and denser modes of the Universal Substance. Then, on the principle of Vibration, the less dense the substance in which the Life is immersed, the more it must be subject to being stirred by vibratory currents other than those produced by the conscious action of the Ego, or inherent Life, of the individuality that is being formed.

But "*the Sum of the Vibrations in anything determines the mode, power, and direction of its action*"; therefore, the less the Ego be concentrated through association with a dense vehicle, the more "wobbly" it must be, and consequently the less able to take any effective part in the further work of Creation. But in proportion as the Ego builds up an *Individual Will*, the more it gets out of the "wobbly" state—or, to refer once more to the idea of etheric waves—it becomes able to select what vibrations it will receive, and what vibrations it will send out.

The involution of the Ego into the physical body, such as we at present know it, is therefore a necessity of the case, if any effective Individuality is to be brought into existence, and the work of Creation carried on instead of being cut short, not for want of material, but for want of workmen capable of using the tools of the builders' craft—the Law as "Strength" and the Word as "Beauty."

The Descending Arc of the Circle of Being is therefore that of the Involution of Spirit into denser and denser modes of Substance,—a process called in technical language by the Greek name "Eleusin," and the process continues until a point is reached where Spirit and Substance are in equal balance, which is where we are now. Then comes the tug of war. Which of the two is to predominate? They are the Expansive and Constrictive primal elements, the "rouah" and "hoshech" of the Hebrew Genesis.

If the Constrictive element be allowed to go further than giving necessary form to the Expansive element, it imprisons the latter. The condensation becomes too dense for the Ego to receive or send forth vibrations according to its free will, and so the Individuality becomes lost. If the condensation process be not carried far enough, no Individuality can be built up, and if it be carried too far, no Individuality can emerge; so in both cases we get the same result that there is no one to speak the Word of Power without which "Nature unaided fails."

Thus we are now exactly at the bottom of the Circle of Being. We have completed the Descending Arc and reached the point where the realization of the Distinctness of Conscious Individuality enables us to choose our own line, whether that of progressing through the stages of the Ascending Arc of Being, or of falling out from the living Circle of Progression, at least for a period, into what is sometimes mystically spoken of as "the Moon," or (in descending order) the "Eighth Sphere," and which is called in Scripture "The Outer Darkness," — the rigidity which stops the action of Life.

Therefore it is with regard to this stage of our career that the Bible lays so much stress on the conflict between the Spirit and the Flesh — it is a fact in the course of our evolution, and the purpose of the Bible is to teach us how to move forward along the Ascending Arc of the Circle of Being, so as to build up individualities which will be able to use the tools of Intelligence and Will in the great work of Evolution, both Personal and Cosmic.

Now what is shown diagrammatically as the Ascending Arc of the Circle of Life is the Return from its lowest point, or the *Full Consciousness of Personal Distinctness*, gained through *the Material Body*, back to its highest point or the Originating Life itself. This is the truth embodied in the parable of the Prodigal Son. It is a Cosmic truth, and this return journey is technically called by the Green name "Anaktorion." It is the Rising-again, that is from matter to Spirit, and is the Resurrection Principle.

But what is accomplished by the journey of the Ego round the Circle of Life?

A New Centre of Intelligence and volition is established; from this the Creative Word of Power can be spoken — a *Complete Man* has been brought into existence, who can take a *free and intelligent* part in the further work of Creation, by his understanding of the interaction between the Law and the Word. The "Volume of the Sacred Law" lies open before us, and the Vibratory Power of the Word to give effect to it is the "Blazing Star" that illuminates its contents, and so we become fellow-workers with the Great Architect of the Universe.

For these reasons it appears to me that our self-recognition in a physical body is a necessary step in our growth. But why should the reconstruction of a physical body be either necessary or desirable? The answer is as follows:

Obviously self-recognition is the necessary basis for all use of those powers of selection and volition by which the Impersonal Law is to be specialized so as to bring to light its limitless potentialities; and self-recognition means the recognition of our personal Distinctness from our environment. Therefore it must always mean the possessing of a body as a vehicle, by means of which to act upon that environment, and to receive the corresponding reaction from it. In other words it must always be a body constituted in terms of the plane upon which we are functioning. But it does not follow that we should always be tied down to one plane.

On the contrary, the very conception of the power of the Word to specialize the action of the Law, implies the power of functioning on any plane we choose; but always subject to the Law, that if we want to act on any particular plane in *propria persona*, and not merely by influencing some other agent, we can only do so by assuming a body in terms of the nature of that plane. Therefore, if we want to act on the physical plane, we must put on a physical body. But when we have fully grasped the Power of the Word we cannot be tied to a body. We shall no longer regard it as composed of so many chemical elements, but we shall see beyond them into the real primary etheric substance of which they are composed, and so by our volition shall be able to put the physical body on or off at pleasure,—that at least is a quite logical deduction from what we have learnt in the preceding pages.

Seen in this light the "Resurrection Body" is not the old body resuscitated, but a new body, just as real and tangible as the old one, only not subject to any of its disabilities,—no longer a limitation, but the ever ready instrument for any work we may desire to do upon the physical plane.

But perhaps you will say, "Why should we want to have anything more to do with the physical plane? surely we have had enough of it already!" Yes; in its old sense of limitation; but not in the new sense of a world of glorious possibilities, a new field for our creative activities; not the least of which is the helping of those who are still in those lower stages which we have already passed through.

I think if we realize the position of the Fully Risen Man, we shall see that he is not likely to turn his back upon the Earth as a rotten, old thing. Therefore a new physical body is a necessary part of his equipment.

If, then, we take it as a general principle, that for self-recognition upon any plane a body in terms of that plane is a necessity, this will throw some light on the Bible narrative of our Lord's appearances after his Resurrection. It is noteworthy that he himself lays stress on the body as an integral part of the individuality. When the disciples thought they had seen an apparition he said: "Handle me and see that it is I *myself*, and *not* a spirit, for a spirit hath not flesh and bones as ye see I have" (Luke xxiv, 39). This very clearly states that the spirit without a corresponding body is not the complete "I myself"; yet from the same narrative we gather that the solid body in which he appeared is able to pass through closed doors, and to be disintegrated and re-integrated at will. Now on the electronic theory of the constitution of matter which I have spoken of in the earlier part of this book, there is nothing impossible in this; on the contrary it is only the known Law of synchronous vibration carried into those further ranges of wave-lengths which, though not yet produced by laboratory experiment, are unavoidably recognized by the mathematicians.

In this way then the Resurrection of the Body appears to me to be the legitimate termination of our present stage of existence. What further developments may follow, who shall say? for we must remember that the end of one series is always the commencement of another—that is the doctrine of the Octave. But this is far enough to look forward in all conscience. As to *when* the completion of our present stage of evolution will be attained, it is impossible even to hazard a guess; but that the *individual* attainment of such a Resurrection is not dependent on any particular date in the world's history, is clearly the teaching of Scripture. When Martha said to Jesus that she knew her brother would rise again "at the last day," he ignored the question of "the last day," and said "I am the Resurrection and the Life" (St. John xi, 25); and similarly St. Paul puts it forward as a thing to be attained (Ph. iii, 15). It is not a resurrection *of* the dead but *from among* the dead that St. Paul is aiming at—not an "anastasis ton nekron," but an "anastasis *ek* ton nekron."

Doubtless there are other passages of Scripture which speak of a general resurrection, which to some will be a resurrection to condemnation (St. John v, 29), a resurrection to shame and everlasting contempt (Dan. xii, 2). This is a subject upon which I will not attempt to enter—I have a great many things to learn, and this is one of them; but if the Bible statements regarding resurrection are to be taken as a whole, these passages cannot be passed over without notice. On the other hand the Bible statements regarding *individual* resurrection are there also, and the general principle on which they are based becomes clear when we see the fundamental relation between the Law and the Word. Only we must remember that the Word that can thus set in motion the Law of Life, and make it triumph over the Law of Death, cannot be spoken by the limited personality which only knows itself as John Smith or Mary Jones. We must attain a larger personality than that, before we can speak the Word. And this larger personality is not just John Smith or Mary Jones magnified; that is the mistake we are all so apt to fall into. Mere magnification will not do it. A square will continue to be a square however large you make it; it will never become a circle. But on the other hand, there is such a thing as stating the area of a circle in the form of a square; and when we learn to regard our square as not existing on its own account, but as an expression of the circle in another form, our attention will be directed to the circle first, as the generating figure, and *then* to the square as a particular mode of expressing the same area. If we look at it in this way we shall never mistake the square for the circle, but we shall see that as the circle grows, the corresponding square will grow with it. It is this dependence of the square on the circle that makes all the difference, and makes it a living, growing square. For the true circle represents Infinitude. It is not bounded by a limiting circumference as in the merely symbolic geometrical figure, but is rather represented by the impulse which generates an ever widening circle of electromagnetic waves; and when we realize this, our square becomes a living thing. The "Word" that we speak with this recognition is no longer ours, but His who sent us—the expression, on the plane of individuality, of the Thought that sent us into existence and so it is the "Word of Life." This is the true Resurrection of the Individual.

CHAPTER VIII

TRANSFERRING THE BURDEN

The more we grow into a clear perception of what is really meant by "Squaring the Circle," the freer we shall find ourselves from the burden of anxiety. We shall rise to a larger generalization of the Law of Cause and Effect. We shall learn in all things to reach out to First Cause as operating through the channels of secondary causation,—"causa causas" as producing, and therefore controlling "causa causata"—and so we cease to worry about secondary causes. On the plane of the lower personality we see certain facts, and argue that they are bound to produce certain results, which would be quite true if we really saw *all* the facts; or, again, allowing that in any particular case we actually did see all the facts as they now exist, we can either deny the operation of First Cause, or recognize its infinite capacity for creating new facts. Therefore, whatever may be the nature of our anxiety, we should endeavour to dispel it by the consideration that there may be already existing other facts we do not know of, which will produce a different result from the one we fear, and that in any case there is a power which can produce new facts in answer to our appeal to it.

But I can imagine some one saying to us, "You bumptious little midget, do you think First Cause is going to trouble Itself about you and your petty concerns? Do you not know that First Cause works by universal Law, and makes no exceptions?" Well, I would not have written this book if I did not suppose that First Cause works by universal Law, and it is just because It does so that I believe It *will* work for me and my concerns. The Law makes no exceptions, but it can be specialized through the power of the Word. Then our sceptic says, "What, do you think *your* word can do that?" To which I reply, "It is not my word because I am not using it in my lower personality, as John Smith or Mary Jones, but in that higher personality which recognizes only one all-embracing Personality and itself as included in that."

Which comes first, the Law or the Word?

The distribution of the solar systems in space, the localization of the Spirit in specific areas of cosmic activity, proclaims the starting of all manifestation through the "Word." Then the operation of Law follows with mathematical precision, just as when we write 2 × 2 we cannot avoid getting 4 as the result—only there is no reason why we should not write 2 × 3 and so get 6 instead of 4. Let it be borne in mind that the Law flows from the Word, and not *vice versa,* and you have got the clue to the enigma of Life.

How far we shall be able to make practical use of this clue depends, of course, on our acceptance of its principle.

The Directing Power of the Word is *inherent* in the Word, and we cannot alter it. *It is the Law* OF *the Law,* and so, like any other law, it cannot be broken, but its action can be inverted. We cannot deprive the Word of its efficacy, but our denial of it as the Word of Expansion is equivalent to an affirmation of it as the Word of Contraction, and so the Law acts towards us as a Limitation. But the fault is not in the Law, but in the way we use the Word. Now if the reader grasps this, he will see that the less we trouble ourselves about what appear to us to be the visible and calculable causes of things, the freer we must become from the burden of anxiety; and as we advance step by step to a clearer recognition of the true order of Cause and Effect, so all intermediate causes will fade from our view. Only the two extremes of the sequence of Cause and Effect will remain in sight. First Cause, moving as the Word, starting a sequence, and the desired result terminating it, as the Word taking Form in Fact. The intermediate links in the chain will be there, but they will be seen as effects, not causes. The wider the generalization we thus make, the less we shall need to trouble about particulars, knowing that they will form themselves by the natural action of the Law; and the widest generalization is therefore, to state not what we want to *have,* but what we want to *be.* The only reason we ever want to *have* anything, is because we think it will help us to be something—something more than we are now; so that the "having" is only a link in the chain of secondary causes, and may therefore be left out of consideration, for it will come of itself through the natural workings of the Law, set in operation by the Word as First Cause. This principle is set forth in the statement of the Divine Name given to Moses (Ex. iii, 13-14). The Name is simply "I AM"—it is Being, not having—the having follows as a natural consequence of the Being; and if it be true that we are made in the likeness and image of God, that is to say on the same Principle, then what is the Law of the Divine nature must be the Law of ours also—and as we awake to this we become "partakers of the Divine Nature" (2 Pet. i, 4).

What we really want, therefore, is to *be* something—something more than we are now; and this is quite right. It is our consciousness of the continually generative impulse of the Eternal Living Spirit, which is the *fons et origo* (fountain and source) of all differentiated life working within us for ever more and more perfect individual expression of all that is in Itself. If the reader remembers what I said at the beginning of this book about the Verb Substantive of Being, he will see that each of us is in truth a "Word (verbum) of God." Let not the orthodox reader be shocked at this—I am only saying what the Bible does. Look up the following passages: "I will write upon him the name of my God and my own new name" (Rev. xiii, 12). "I saw, and behold a lamb standing on the Mount Zion (note, the word Zion means the principle of Life), and with him a hundred and forty and four thousand, having his name and the name of his Father written on their foreheads" (Rev. xiv, 1). "His name shall be on their foreheads" (Rev. xxii, 4). Read particularly the whole passage Rev. xix, 11-16, where we are expressly told that the name in question is "the Word of God"; and that this name is the one put upon those who follow their Leader, is shown by the same description being given of the followers as of the Leader. They all ride upon "white horses," and the "horse" is the symbol of the intellect. Also in the case of the Leader, the peculiarity of his Name is that "no one knows it but himself," and in Rev. ii, 17, exactly the same thing is said of the "New Name" to be given "to him that overcometh." Again, in Isaiah lxii, 2, "Thou shalt be called by a new name, which the mouth of the Lord shall name"; and again in Num. vi, 27, "They shall put my name upon the children of Israel."

Then as the meaning of that Name "the Word of God." In Ps. cxix, 160: "Thy word is true from the beginning," and Jesus said: "Thy Word is Truth" (John xvii, 17).

This also corresponds with the description in Rev. xix, 11-16 where another name for "the Word of God" is "Faithful and True"; and the same metaphor of the Truth "*riding into action*" is contained in Ps. xlv, 3, 4. "Gird thy sword upon thy thigh, O most mighty, with thy glory and thy majesty; and in thy majesty ride prosperously because of Truth." The same symbol of "riding" also occurs in Ps. lxviii: "Extol him that rideth upon the heavens," "Sing praises to him that rideth upon the heaven of heavens which were of old (i.e., *ab initio*); lo, he doth send out his Voice and that a mighty Voice"—and the word "Voice" is the Hebrew Word [Hebrew: "K[=o]l"], meaning "Sound" or "Word"—so that here again we have the idea of "The Word" riding into action. Once more—"Thou hast magnified thy Word above all thy Name" (Ps. cxxxviii, 2), thus repeating the idea of the Word as the Name.

In other passages we have the idea of the Word as a Weapon. "The Sword of the Spirit which is the Word of God" (Eph. vi, 17), which answers to the description in Revelations of the Sword proceeding out of the mouth of the Word; and we have the same metaphor of the Word riding into action in Habakkuk iii, 8 and 9. "Thou didst ride upon thine horses and thy chariots of salvation. Thy bow was made quite naked ... even thy Word"; and similarly those that oppose the Word are "killed with the sword of him that sat upon the horse, which sword proceeded out of his mouth."

In other passages we have the Word put before us as a Defence. "His Truth shall be thy shield and buckler" (Ps. xci, 4); and again "The Name of the Lord is a strong tower; the righteous runneth into it and is safe" (Prov. xviii, 10); and we have already seen that this Name is "The Word of God"; and similarly in Ps. cxxiv, 8: "Our help is in the name of the Lord, who made heaven and earth."

Lastly, we get "the Word" as the final deliverance from all ill; "Into thy hand I commit my spirit: thou hast redeemed me, O Lord God of Truth" (Ps. xxxi, 5).

And the reason of all this is because "His Truth endureth to all generations" (Ps. c, 5); it is everlasting, Changeless Principle. "By the

Word of the Lord were the heavens made; and all the host of them by the breath of his mouth" (Ps. xxxiii, 6), as is also said of the Word in the opening of St. John's Gospel and First Epistle.

Now a careful comparison of these and similar passages will make it clear that the sequence presented to us is as follows: The "Word" is the passing of the Verb Substantive of Being into Action. It is always the same in Principle, on whatever scale, and therefore applies to ourselves also, so that each one of us is a "Word of God." We are this by the very essence of our being, and that is why the first thing we are told about Man is, that he is made in the image and likeness of God. But how far any of us will become a really effective "Word," depends upon our acceptance of the New Name which is ready to be bestowed upon each one. "To as many as *receive* him, to them gives he power to become Sons of God, even to them that believe on his Name" (John 1-12). We get the New Name by realizing the Truth, which Truth is that we ourselves are included in THE NAME, and that name is called "The Word of God."

The meaning of which becomes clear if we remember that the spiritual name of anything is its "Noumenon" or essential being, which is manifested through its "Phenomenon" or outward reproduction in Form; so that the true order is first our "Name" or essential Being, then our "Word" or active manifestation of this essential Being, then the "Truth" or the unchangeable Law of Being passing into Manifestation—and these three are ONE. Then when we see that this is true of ourselves, not because of some arbitrary favouritism making us exceptions to the human race, but because it is the working on the plane of Human Individuality of the same Power and the same Law by which the world has come into existence, we can see that we have here a Principle which we can trust to work as infallibly as the principle of Mathematics; and that therefore the desire to become something more than we now are is nothing else than the Eternal Spirit of Life seeking ever fuller expression.

The correction which our mode of thinking needs therefore is to start with Being, not with Having, and we may then trust the Having to come along in its right order; and if we can get into this new manner of thinking, what a world of worry it will save us! If we realize that the Law flows from the Word, and not vice versa, then the Law of attraction must work in this manner, and will bring to us all those conditions through which we shall be able to express the more expanded Being towards which we are directing our Word; and as a consequence, we shall have no need to trouble about forcing particular conditions into existence—they will grow spontaneously out of the seed we have planted. All we have to do now, or at any time, is to take the conditions that are ready to hand and use them on the lines of the sort of "being" towards which we are directing our Thought—use them just as far as they go at the time, without trying to press them further—and we shall find by experience that out of the present conditions thus used to-day, more favourable conditions will grow in a perfectly natural manner to-morrow, and so on, day by day, until, when later on we look back, we shall be surprised to find ourselves expressing all, and more than all, the sort of "*being*" we had thought of. Then, from this new standpoint of our being, we shall continue to go on in the same way, and so on *ad infinitum,* so that our life will become one endless progress, ever widening as we go on. And this will be found a very quiet and peaceful way, free from worry and anxiety, and wonderfully effective. It may lead you to some position of authority or celebrity; but as such things belong to the category of "Having" and not of "Being" they were not what you aimed at, and are only by-products of what you have become in yourself. They are conditions, and like all other conditions should be made use of for the development of still more expanded "being"; that is to say, you will go on working on the more extended scale which such a position makes possible to you. But the one thing you would not try to do with it would be to "boss the show." The moment you do this you are no longer using the Word of the larger Personality, and have descended to your old level of the smaller personality, just John Smith or Mary Jones, ignorant of yourselves as being anything greater. It is true your Word still directs the operation of the Law towards yourself—it always does this—but your word has become inverted, and so calls into operation the Law of Contraction instead of the Law of Expansion. A higher position means a wider field for usefulness—that is all; and to the extent to which you fit yourself for it, it will come to you. So, if you content yourself with always speaking in your Thought the Creative Word of "Being" from day to day, you will find it the Way of Peace and the Secret of a Happy Life—by no means monotonous, for all sorts of unexpected interests will be continually opening out to you, giving you scope for all the activities of which your present degree of "being" renders you capable. You will always find plenty to do, and find pleasure in doing it, so you need never be afraid of feeling dull.

But perhaps you will say:

"How am I to know that I am not speaking my own Word instead of that of the Creative Spirit?"

Well, the word of the smaller personality is always based on the idea of possessing, and the Word of the Spirit is always based on the idea of Becoming—that is the criterion. And also, if we base our speaking of the Word on the Promises of Spirit, we may be sure that we are on the right track.

We may be sure of it, because when we come to analyze these promises we shall find that they are all statements of the Creative Law of Being, and the nature of this Law is obvious from the facts of the Visible Creation.

These things are not true because they are written in the Bible, but the Bible is true because these things are written in it. The more we examine the Bible Promises, the more they will impress themselves upon us as being Promises according to Law; and since the Law can never be broken, we can feel quite secure of it, subject to the one condition that we do not stop the Law from working to the fulfilment of the Promise, by our own inverted use of the Word. But if we take the *Word of the Promise* and make it our own Word, then we know that we are speaking the right Word, which will so specialize the action of the Law, as to produce the fulfilment of the Promise. Apart from the Word there is no Foundation. In all other systems we have either Law without Will, or Will without Law.

Then we know that we are not speaking of ourselves, but are speaking the Word of the Power that sent us into the World. The Law alone cannot fulfil the Promises. It is in itself Cosmic and Impersonal, and, as every scientific discovery amply demonstrates, it needs the co-operation of the Personal Factor to bring out its latent possibilities; so that the Word is as necessary as the Law for the fulfilment of the Promises; but if the Word which we speak is that of the Creating Spirit, we may reckon it as being just as certain in its operation as the Law, and the two together form an infallible Power.

But there is one thing we must not forget, and this is the Law of Growth. If the Law which we plant is the seed, then we must allow time for it to grow; we must leave it alone and go about our business as usual, and the seed we have sown will spring and grow up of itself, we know not how, a truth which we have been told by the Master himself (Mark iv, 26, 29).

We must not be like children who plant a seed one day, and dig it up the next to see whether it is growing. Our part is to plant the seed, not to make it grow,—the Creative Law of Life will do that. It is for this reason that the Bible gives us such injunctions as "Study to be quiet" (1 Thess. iv, 11). "He that believeth shall not make haste" (Is. xxviii, 16). "In quietness and in confidence shall be your strength" (Is. xxx, 15). To make ourselves anxious as to whether the Word we have planted will fructify is just to dig it up again, and then of course it will not grow.

The fundamental maxim, then, which we must always keep in mind is that "Every creation carries its own Mathematics along with it," and that therefore "The Law flows from the Word, and not *vice versa;*" and consequently "*The Word is the Foundation of every creative series,*" whether that series be great or small, cosmic or individual, constructive or destructive. Every series commences with Intention; and remember the exact meaning of the Word. It is from the two Latin words "in," towards, and "tendere," to stretch, and it therefore means a "reaching out in a certain direction." This "reaching out in a certain direction" is the Conception of ourself as arrived at the destination towards which our Thought tends, and is therefore *the conceiving of an idea,* and our formulated idea is stated, if only mentally, in Words—and the termination of the series is the realization of the idea in actual fact. Therefore it is equally true of every series, whether it be the creation of a lady's blouse or the creation of a world, that "in the Beginning is the Word"—the Word is *the Point of Origination.*

Then, since the Word is the Point of Origination, what is our conception of the best thing we can originate with it? There is a great variety of opinion as to what is desirable; and it is only natural and right that it should be so, for otherwise we should be without any individuality, which means that we should have no real life in us—in fact such a world is unthinkable; it would be a world that had ceased to move, it would be a dead world. So it is the varied conception of "the Good" that makes the world go on. Uniformity means reducing things to one dead level. But on the other hand there must be Unity—unity of action resulting from unity of purpose, otherwise the world logically terminates in internecine strife. If then the world is to go on, it can only be by means of Unity expressing itself in Variety, and therefore the question is: What is the *unifying Desire* which underlies all the varieties of expression? It is a very simple one—it is just to ENJOY LIVING. Our ideas of an enjoyable life may be very various, but that is what we all really want; so what we want to get at is: What is the basis of an enjoyable life?

I have no hesitation in saying that the secret of enjoying life is *to take an interest in it*. The opposite of Livingness is Deadness, that is, inertia and stagnation. Dying of "ennui" is a very real thing indeed, and if we would not die of this malady we must have an interest in life that will always keep going on.

Now for anything to interest us we must enter into the spirit of it. If we do not enter into the spirit of a game it does not interest us; if we do not enter into the spirit of a book, it does not interest us, we are bored to death with it; and so on with everything. So from our own experience we may lay down the maxim that "To enjoy anything we must enter into the spirit of it," and if this be so, then, to enjoy the "Living Quality of Life" we must enter into the Spirit of Life itself. I say the "Living Quality of Life" so as to dissociate it from all ideas of particular conditions; because what we are trying to get at is the fundamental principle of Life which creates conditions, and not the reflex of sensations, whether physical or mental, which any particular set of conditions may induce in us for the time being. In this way we come back to the initial proposition with which we started—that the origin of everything is only to be found in a Universal Ever-Living Spirit, and that our own life proceeds from this Spirit in accordance with the maxim "Omne vivum ex vivo." Thus we are logically brought to the conclusion that the ultimate Desire of all Humanity is to consciously enter into the Spirit of

Life as it is *in itself*, antecedently to all conditions. This is the widest of all generalizations, and so opens the door to the highest of all specializations; for it is a scientific fact that the more widely we can generalize the principle of any Law, the more highly we can specialize its working. It is only as our conception of it is limited that any Law limits us.

A principle *per se* is always undifferentiated, and capable of any sort of differentiation into particular modes of expression that are not in opposition to the principle itself; and it is true of the Principle of Life as of all others. There is therefore no limit to its expression except that which inverts it,—that is to say, anything which tends towards Death; and, accordingly, what we have to avoid is the negative mode of Thought, which starts an inverted action of the Law, logically resulting in destructiveness instead of constructiveness. But the mistake we make from not seeing the basic principle of the whole thing, is that of looking to the conditions to form the Life, instead of looking to the Life to form the conditions; and therefore what we require is a *Standard of Measurement* for our Thought, by which we shall be able to form *The Perfect Word* which will set in motion the Law of Cause and Effect in such a manner as to fulfil that *Basic Desire of Life* which is common to all Humanity. The Perfect Word must therefore fulfil two Conditions—it must have the essential Quality of the Undifferentiated Eternal Life, and it must have the essential Quality of "Genus Homo." It must say with Horace "Homo sum; nihil humani mihi alienum puto" (I am Man; I regard nothing human as alien to myself). When we think it out carefully, there is no escaping the conclusion that this must be the essential Quality of the Perfect Word we are in search of. It is the final logical inference from all that we have learnt regarding the interaction between Law and Personality, that the Perfect Word must combine in itself the Quality of each—it must be at once both Human and Divine.

Of course all my readers know where the description of such a Word is to be found; but what I want them to realize is the way in which we have now reached a similar description of the Perfect Word. We have not accepted it unquestioningly as the teaching of a scholastic theology, but have arrived at it by a course of careful reasoning from the facts of physical Nature and from our experience of our own mental powers. This way of getting at it makes it really our own. We know what we mean by it, and it is no longer a mere traditional form of words. It is the same with everything else; nothing becomes our own by being just told about it.

For instance, if I show an artist a picture, and he tells me that a boat in it is half a mile away from the spectators, I may accept this on his authority, because I suppose he knows all about it. But if next day a friend shows me a picture of a bit of coast with a fishing-boat in the distance, and asks me how far off that boat is, I am utterly stumped because I do not know how the artist was able to judge the distance. But if I understand the principle, I give my friend a very fair approximation of the distance of the boat. I work it out like this. I say:—the immediate foreground of the picture shows an amount of detail which could not be seen more than twenty yards away, and the average size of such details in nature shows that the bottom edge of the picture must measure about ten yards across. Then from experience I know that the average length of craft of the particular rigging in the picture is, say, about eighty feet, and I then measure that this length goes sixteen and a half times across the picture on the level where the boat is situated, and so I know that a line across the picture at this level measures 80 x 16-1/2 = 1320 ft. = 440 yards. Then I make the calculation: 10 yds.: 440 yds.:: 20 yds.: the distance required to be ascertained 440 x 20 / 10 = 880 yds. 1760 yds. = 1 mile and 1760 / 2 = 880 yds. Therefore I know that the boat in the picture is represented as being about half a mile from the spectator. I really know the distance and do not merely guess it, and I know *how* I know it. I know it simply from the geometrical principle that with a given angle at the apex of a triangle the length of a perpendicular dropped from the apex to the base of the triangle will always bear the same ratio to the length of the base, whatever the size of the triangle may be. In this way I know the distance of the boat in the picture by combining mathematics and my own observation of facts—once again to co-operation of Law and Personality. Now a familiar instance like this shows the difference between being told a thing and really knowing it, and it is by an analogous method that we have now arrived at the conclusion that the Perfect Word is a combination of the Human and the Divine. We have definite reasons for seeing this as the ultimate fact of human development—the power to give expression to the Perfect Word—, and that this follows naturally from the fact of our own existence and that of some originating source from which we derive it.

But perhaps the reader will say: How can a Word take form as a Person? Well, words which do not eventually take form as facts only evaporate into thin air, and we cannot conceive the Divine Ideals of Man doing this. Therefore the expression of the Perfect Word on the plane of Humanity must take substance in the Form of Humanity. It is not the manifestation of any limited personality with all his or her idiosyncrasies, but the manifestation of the basic principle of Humanity itself common to us all.

To quote Dryden's words—but in a very different sense to that intended in "Absolom and Achitophel,"—such a one must be "Not one, but all Mankind's epitome." The manifestation must be the Perfect Expression of that fundamental Life which is the Root Desire in us all, and which is therefore called "The Desire of all nations."

Here then we have reached (Haggai ii, 7) the foundation fact of Human Personality. It is the Eternal "Will-to-live," as Schopenhauer calls it, which works subconsciously in all creation; therefore it is the root from which all creation springs. In the atom it becomes atomic energy, in the plant it becomes vegetable life, in the animal it becomes animal life, and in man it becomes personal life, and therefore, if a Perfect Standard of the Eternal Life is to be set before us, it must be in terms of Human Personality.

But some one will say: Why should we need such a Standard? The answer is that since the working of the Law towards each of us is determined by our mode of Thought, we require to be guarded against an inverted use of the Word. "Ignorantia Legis nemini excusat" (ignorance of the Law does not excuse you from its operation), is a scientific, as well as a forensic maxim, for the Law of Cause and Effect can never be altered. Our ignorance of the laws of electricity will not prevent us from being electrocuted if we get into the circuit of some powerful voltage.

Therefore, because the Law is *Impersonal* and knows no exceptions, and will bring us either Life or Death according to the direction which we give it by our Word, it is of the first importance for us to have a Standard by which to measure the Word expressed through our own Personality. This is why St. Paul speaks of our growing to "the measure of the stature of the fulness of Christ," (Eph. iv, 13) and why we find the symbol of "Measurement" so frequently employed in the Bible.

Therefore, if a great scale of measurement for our Word is to be exhibited, it can only be by its presentation in human form.

Then if the purpose be to establish such a standard of measurement, the scale must be expressed in units of the same denomination as that of our own nature—you cannot divide miles by ampères—and it is because the scale of our potential being is laid out in the same denomination as that of the Spirit of Life itself that we can avail ourselves of the standard of "the Word made Flesh."

When this is clearly seen it removes those intellectual difficulties which so many feel with regard to the doctrine of the Atonement. If we want to avail ourselves of the Bible Promises on the basis of the Bible teaching, we cannot throw the teaching overboard. As I have said before, if a doctrine is to be rightly interpreted, it must be interpreted as a whole, and in one form or another the doctrine of the Atonement is the pivot point of the whole Bible. To omit it is like trying to play "Hamlet" with Hamlet left out, and you may put your Bible out on the rubbish-heap. How, then, does the Atonement come in?

Here are the usual intellectual difficulties. To whom is the sacrifice offered? To God or to the Devil? If it be to the Devil, then the Devil is a greater power than God. If it be to God, then how can a God who demands a sacrifice of blood be Love? And in either case how can guilt be transferred from one person to the other?

Now as a matter of fact none of these questions arise. They are beside the real point at issue, which is: How can we so combine the Personal action of the Word with the Impersonal action of the Law, as to make the Law become to us the Law of Life instead of the Law of Death (Rom. viii, 2)?

Let us recur to the principles which we have worked out. The Law flows from the Word and not *vice versa*—it acts for good or ill according to the Quality of the Word which calls it into action. Therefore to get the Law of Life we must speak the Word of Life.

Then, on the principle of "Omne vivum ex vivo," the Word of Fundamental Basic Life, which is not subject to conditions because it is antecedent to all conditions, can only be spoken through consciousness of participating in the Eternal Life which is the "fons et origo" of all particular being. Therefore, to be able to speak this Word we must have a foundation of assurance that we are in no way separated from the Eternal Life, and since this foundation is required for all men, it must be broad enough to accommodate all grades of perceptions.

Theologically the separation from the Eternal Life is said to be caused by "Sin." But what do we mean by "Sin"?

We can only judge of what a thing *is* by what it *does;* and so, if "Sin" is that which prevents the inflowing of the Eternal Life, which we know is the root of our individual being, then it must be the transgression of the inherent Law of our own Being. The truth is that we live simultaneously in two worlds, the visible and the invisible, just as trees draw their life from the earth beneath and from the air and light above, and the transgression consists in limiting ourselves only to the lower world, and thereby cutting ourselves off from the essential part of our own life, that which *really lives*.

We do not realize the true function of the three lower principles of our nature, viz.: Vital Spirit, etheric body, and outward form; the function of which is to give concentration to the current of spiritual life flowing from the Eternal Spirit, and thus enable the undifferentiated Life to differentiate itself into Individual Consciousness, which will be able to specialize the action of the Law into higher manifestations than it can produce without the co-operation of Personality.

On the analogy of Ohm's Law our error is making our "*R*" so rigid that it ceases to be a conductor, and so no current is delivered and no work done. This is the true nature of sin, and it is this opposition of our *R* to E.M.F. or Eternal Motive Force that has to be removed. We have to realize the true function of our R, as the channel through which the E.M.F. is enabled to carry on its work. When we awake to the fact that our true place in the Order of the Universe is to be fellow-workers with God in carrying on the work of Creation, then we see that hitherto we have entirely missed the purpose of our calling, and have misused the Divine image in which we were created; and therefore we want an assurance that our past errors will not stand in the way of our future advance into continually fuller participation in the Divine Creative Work, which, in virtue of our true nature should be our rightful inheritance.

That our future destiny is to actually take an individual part, however small, in guiding the great work of Evolution, may not be evident to us in the earlier stages of our awakening; but what is clear as a matter of feeling, but not yet intellectually, is, that in some way or other we have been cutting ourselves off from the Great Source of Light, and that what we therefore want, is to be re-united to it. What is wanted, then, is something which will give us a firm ground of assurance that we *are* re-united to it, and that that something must be of such a nature as never to lose anything of its efficiency at any stage of our progress—it must cover the whole ground.

Now, if we think deeply upon this question, we shall gradually come to see that this expansive quality is to be found in the doctrine of the Atonement. It meets all the needs of our spiritual nature in a way that no other theory does, and responds to every stage of our progress. There is only one thing that will prevent it working, and that is, saying that we have no need of it. That is why St. John said, that if we say we have no sin, we deceive ourselves, and the truth is not in us (1 John i, 8). But the more we come into the light of Truth, and realize that sin is everything that is not in accordance with the Law of our own essential being as related to the Eternal Life, the more we shall see, not only that we have transgressed the Law in the past, but also that even now we are very far from completely fulfiling it; and the more light we get the more clearly we shall see this to be the case. Therefore, whatever may be the stage of our mental development, the assurance which we all need for the basis of our new life is that of the removal of sin—the sins of the past, and the daily errors of the present. We may form various theories, each to our own satisfaction, as to *how* this takes place. For instance we may argue that, since "the Word" is the undifferentiated potential of Humanity, every human soul is included in the Self-offering of Christ, and that in Him we ourselves suffered on the Cross. Or we may say that our confession that such an offering is needed amounts to our participation in it. Or we may say with St. Paul that, as in Adam all are sinners, so in Christ all are made free from sin (1 Cor. xv, 22). That is, taking Adam and Christ as the representatives of two orders of men. Or we may fall back on the statement "Sacrifice and burnt offerings Thou wouldst not" (Ps. xl, 6), and on Jesus' own explanation of his death, that He offered himself in testimony to the Truth—that is, that the Eternal Life will no more exercise a retrospective vengeance upon us for our past misunderstanding of It, than would electricity or any other force. We may explain the *modus operandi* of the great offering in any of these ways, for the Scripture presents it in all of them—but the great thing is to accept it; for by the nature of our mental constitution, such an acceptance, whether with or without an intellectual explanation, affords the assurance which we stand in need of; and building upon the Foundation we can safely rear the edifice of our future development.

Also it affords us a continual safeguard in all the further stages of our evolution. As our psychic consciousness increases, we become more and more responsive to psychic stimulus whether that stimulus proceed from a good or evil influence; and therefore the recognition of our Redemption in Christ surrounds us with a protecting barrier, through which no evil spirit or malign influence can pass; so that, resting upon this Truth, we need never be in fear of any such invasion, but shall at all times be clothed with the whole armour of God (Eph. vi, 11).

From whatever point of view we regard it, we therefore find in the One Offering once made for the sin of the whole world, a standpoint such as is provided by no other teaching, whether religious or philosophical; and we shall see on examination that it is not an arbitrary decree for which we can give no account, but that it is based on the psychological constitution of man—a provision so perfectly adapted to our requirements at every stage of our evolution, that we can only attribute it to the Divine Wisdom acting through One, who by Perfect Love, thus willingly offered himself, in order to provide the Foundation of complete assurance for all who recognize their need of it.

On this basis, then, of reunion with the Eternal Source of Life, all the Promises of the Bible are found to be according to Law—that is, according to the inherent Law of our Being; so that, in the laying of this Foundation, we find the supreme manifestation of the interaction between the Law and the Word, which, when its significance is apprehended, opens out vistas of limitless possibilities to the individual and to the race.

But the race, as a whole, is yet very far from apprehending this, and for the most part has no perception of spiritual causation. Where some dim perception of spiritual causation is beginning to emerge, it is very frequently inverted, because people only apprehend it as giving them an additional power of exercising compulsion over their fellow-men, and thus depriving them of that individuality which it is the one purpose of Evolution to develop. This is because people do not look beyond the three lower principles of life, those principles which animals have in common with man; and consequently the higher principle of mind, which distinguishes man, is brought down to the lower level, so that the man is distinguished from the beast only by the possession of intellectual faculties, which by their perversion make him not merely a beast, but a devil of a beast. Therefore the recognition of psychic powers, when not safeguarded by the higher principles of Truth, plunges man even deeper into darkness than does a simple materialism; and so the two go hand in hand on the downward path. There is abundant evidence that this is increasingly the case at the present day; and therefore it is that the Bible Promises culminate in the Promise of the return of Him who offered himself in order to lay the foundation of Peace. As I have said before, we must either take the Bible as a whole, or reject it entirely. We cannot pick and choose what pleases us, and refuse what does not. No legal document could be treated in this way; and in like manner the Bible is one great whole, or else it is just—"skittles."

Therefore, if that Divine "Word" was manifested to save the world from destruction, by opening the way for the *individual* through recognition of his true relation to God, then it is only a reasonable carrying out of the same thought that, when the bulk of mankind fail to realize the beneficent use of these powers, and persist in using them invertedly, the same Being should again appear to save the race from utter self-destruction, but not by the same method, for that would be impossible.

The individual method is that of individual self-recognition in the light of Truth; but that cannot be *forced* upon any one. The headlong downward career of the race as a whole cannot therefore be stopped *vi et armis*, and this can only be done by first letting it have a bitter experience of what intellect, depraved to the service of the Beast in Man, leads to, and then forcibly restraining those who persist in this madness. Therefore a Second Coming of the Divine Man is a logical sequence to the first, and equally logical, this Second Coming must be as One who will rule the nations with irresistible power; so that men, reflecting upon the evils of the past, and enquiring into their cause, may be led to see that cause in the inverted action of the Law of their own being, and may therefore learn so to renew their thoughts in accordance with the Divine Thought as to bring them into the glorious liberty of the Sons of God.

This, then, is the Promise we have to look forward to at the present day, and though it might not be wise to speculate as to the precise time and manner of its fulfilment, there can be no doubt as to the nature of the general principles involved; and I trust the reader has at least learned from this book that principles unfold themselves with unfailing accuracy, though it depends on our Word, or mental attitude, in what way their unfoldment will affect us personally.

For such reasons as these, it appears to me, that the current objections to the doctrine of Atonement are entirely beside the mark. They miss the whole point of the thing. Punishment for Sin? Of course there is punishment for sin so long as it is persisted in. It is the natural working of the Law of Cause and Effect. Forgiveness of sin? Of course there is forgiveness of sin as soon as, through knowledge, we make a right use of the Law of our own Being. It could not be otherwise. It is the natural working of the Law of Cause and Effect.

"This is the covenant that I will make with them after those days, saith the Lord, I will put my laws into their hearts, and in their minds will I write them; and their sins and iniquities will I remember no more" (Heb. x, 16); and similarly in Jer. xxxi, 32, from which the writer of the Epistles to the Hebrews quotes this. "Now the Lord is the Spirit" (2 Cor. iii, 17, R.V.), i.e., the Originating Spirit of life, and therefore "my laws" means the inherent Law of the Originating Principle of Being, so that here we have a plain statement that the realization of the True Law of our Being *ipso facto* results in the cancelling of all our past errors. When once we see the principle of it the whole sequence becomes perfectly plain.

There is nothing arbitrary in all this. It results naturally from a New mode of Thought producing a New order of Consciousness; and it is written that "if any man be in Christ he is a new creature" or, as it says in the margin, "a new creation" (2 Cor. v, 17), and on the principle that "every Creation carries its own mathematics with it," every such man has passed from the Law of Death into the Law of Life. The full fruition may not yet be visible—we must allow for the Law of Growth—but the Principle is in him and has become the central, generating point of his consciousness, and is therefore bound, sooner or later, to develop into perfect manifestation by the Law of its own nature. If the Principle be accepted it will work all the same, whether we accept it by simple trust in the written Word, or whether we analyze the grounds of our trust; just as an electric bell will ring when you press the button, whether you are an electrical engineer or not. But there will be this difference, that if you *are* an electrical engineer you will see the principle implied in the ringing of the bell, and you will find in it the promise of infinite possibilities which it is open to you to develope; and in like manner, the more clearly you see the relation which necessarily exists between yourself and the All-Originating Living Spirit, the more clear it will become to you, that this relation opens up an endless vista of boundless potentialities which can never be exhausted. This is the true nature of the Bible Promises; they were not made by some external Deity about whose ideas we can never have any certainty, but by the Indwelling God, who is at once the Life, the Law, and the Substance of all things, and therefore they are Promises according to Law, containing in themselves the principle of their own fulfilment.

But, as I trust the reader is now convinced, the Law can fulfil the Promise which is latent in it only by the co-operation of the Word; that is, the Personal Factor which provides the necessary conditions for the Law to work under; and therefore, if the Promise is to be fulfilled, we must meet the All-originating Life, the "Premium mobile," not only on the Plane of Law, but on the Plane of Personality also. This becomes evident if we consider that this Originating Life must be *entirely undifferentiated* in Itself; for otherwise it could not be the origin of all differentiated modes of Life and Energy. As long as we find differentiation, on however wide a scale, we have not arrived at First Cause. There will still be something further back, out of which the differentiations have proceeded; and it is this "Something" which is at the back of "Everything" that we are in search of. Therefore the Originating Spirit must be *absolutely undifferentiated,* and consequently the Personal Factor in ourselves must be the differentiation into individuality of a Quality eternally subsisting in the All-Originating Undifferentiated Spirit.

Then, since our individual differentiation of this Quality must depend on the mode of our recognition of it, it follows that a Standard of Measurement is needed, and the Standard is presented to us in the form of the Personality around whom the whole Bible centres, and who, as the Standard of the Divine Infinitude differentiating Himself into units of individual personality, can only be described as at once The Son of God and The Son of Man. If we see that the Eternal Life, by reason of its non-differentiation in itself, must needs become to each of us *exactly what we take it to be,* then it follows that in order to realize it on our own plane of Personality we must see it *through the medium of Personality,* and it is therefore not a theological figment, but the Supreme Psychological Truth that no man can come to "the Father"—that is, to the Parent Spirit—except through the Son (John xiv, 6).

When we see the reason at the back of it, the Bible becomes a New Book to us, and we learn that the interpretation of it is not to be found in learned commentaries, but in ourselves. Then we find that it is indeed The Book of Promises, not vague and uncertain, but logical and scientific, teaching us how to combine the instrumentality of the Law with the freedom of the Word; so that through the Perfect Word, manifested as the Perfect Man, we reach the Perfect Law, and find that THE PERFECT LAW IS THE LAW OF LIBERTY.

THE END

FOOTNOTES:

[1] For various reasons I am not giving the actual names of places and persons in this story.

[2] "Out of Egypt" by Miss Crouse. Gorham Press, Boston, U.S.A.

[3] R.W. Allen.

[4] See Chapters on "Body, Soul, and Spirit" in my "Edinburgh Lectures on Mental Science."

[5] See "Edinburgh Lectures."

[6] "New Knowledge."